We're back and more hard-boiled than ever.

Call us self-serving, but this time we'd like to thank some of the critics who've supported Old School Books. In case you missed it, here's what a few of them had to say:

Spin: "Walking the mean streets with hearts set on dreams they know damn well they'll never reach, these authors keep it realer than any rapper knows how. . . . They testify to how much was lost when these novelists couldn't get read as seriously as they should have."

The Source: "They take the brutality and ruin of the urban black landscape and transform them into art."

Playboy: "One of the most exciting literary revival series since the rediscovery of Jim Thompson's novels."

Detour: "The Old School will give the modern reader a wake-up slap, alerting them to a subversive canon too long ignored."

Details: "Down-and-dirty tales about real O.G.'s, stories that drop you in the middle of the crumbling inner cities for a street-level view of the black urban experience. . . . If you like the page-turning pulp of Raymond Chandler, James Ellroy, and Jim Thompson, definitely add the Old School to your hard-boiled syllabus."

Time Out: "Unflinching biographies of the streets. . . . a blood-soaked landmark of crime fiction."

USA Today: "Harder than a set of brass knuckles and pulpier than home-squeezed orange juice. . . . With any luck the legacy of the Old School Books writers will not be lost again."

New York Newsday: "The editors have unearthed a motherload of revelation; a shadow tradition of hot-wired prose playing its own variations on noir with bebop abandon and rhythm-and-blues momentum."

Kind words, and don't think we aren't grateful.

While we've got your attention, we'd like to make this important announcement. OSB will soon unveil its first hardcover reissue:

Chester Himes's lost classic, *Cast the First Stone*. Least that's what the world has called it until now. With a little help from some friends, we've restored one hundred (or so) pages from Himes's original manuscript, "dyed" several of the characters black as they were in Himes's earliest editions, and are publishing it under its original title, *Yesterday Will Make You Cry*. We consider it nothing less than a literary revelation—we hope you will too.

Until then, we hope you enjoy our terrific trio of new titles. And be sure to keep those cards and letters coming.

The School on 103rd Street

OLD SCHOOL BOOKS

edited by Marc Gerald and Samuel Blumenfeld

ROLAND S. JEFFERSON

The School on 103rd Street

SB

Old School Books

W · W · Norton & Company
New York · London

Copyright © 1997 by Marc Gerald and Samuel Blumenfeld

Foreword to *The School on 103rd Street* copyright © 1997 by Roland S. Jefferson, M.D.
The School on 103rd Street copyright © 1976 by Roland S. Jefferson, M.D.

The text of this book is composed in Sabon, with the display set in Stacatto 555 and Futura.
Composition by Crane Typesetting Service, Inc.
Manufacturing by Courier Companies, Inc.
Book design by Jack Meserole.

Library of Congress Cataloging-in-Publication Data
Jefferson, Roland S.
　　The school on 103rd Street / by Roland S. Jefferson.
　　　　p.　cm.—(Old school books)
　　ISBN 0-393-31662-9 (pbk.)
　　　I. Title.　II. Series.
PS3560.E415S48　1997
813'.54—dc21　　　　　　　　　　　　　　　　　　　　　　97-5669
　　　　　　　　　　　　　　　　　　　　　　　　　　　　　　CIP

W. W. Norton & Company, Inc., 500 Fifth Avenue, New York, N.Y. 10110
http://www.wwnorton.com

W. W. Norton & Company Ltd., 10 Coptic Street, London WC1A 1PU

1　2　3　4　5　6　7　8　9　0

To:

Cassius
Sol
Danny
Judy
Max

. . . in appreciation for their encouragement and faith.
A very special appreciation to my wife, Melanie, whose devotion
and support helped make this book a reality.

ROLAND S. JEFFERSON

Leonard L'Bey

If you read John A. Williams's *The Angry Ones*, then you're already aware of the fate that befalls ninety-nine out of one hundred books published by a vanity press. For those of you who didn't do your Old School homework, the answer is a fat bill from the publisher and a stillborn book.

Roland Jefferson's unsettling political thriller *The School on 103rd Street* is not only one of the few exceptions, it is, you'll soon see, a damn good read. Turned down by all of the legitimate publishing houses, it was released by the Vantage Press, the unsurpassed king of the vanities, in 1974. "What Vantage didn't realize is that I would publicize it," Jefferson recalls with a laugh. "I took out some radio spots, did some limited ads in the black press." The result: a smattering of appreciative reviews and a soldout first printing.

Having already turned its profit, Vantage opted not to go in for a second run, but four years later the book was briefly revived in paperback by the Holloway House. Based on word of mouth alone, again the book sold out, again the publisher decided not to risk another printing, again the book disappeared.

So who is Roland Jefferson and why does *The School on 103rd Street* warrant another reading? First things first.

Jefferson was born in Washington, D.C., in 1939 and moved to Los Angeles at the age of five. Jefferson says that from his earliest teens he wanted to be a journalist, but his father, in his infinite wisdom, cautioned him against a career in the writing trade. Jefferson listened. After graduating from USC, he received his medical degree from Howard University, served two years as captain in the Air Force, and settled in Los Angeles.

But while his father might have scared him away from a career in writing, he couldn't scare him away from his typewriter—and since the early 1970s, Jefferson has authored a wide range of projects while working full time as a forensic psychiatrist. Highlights: *A Card for the Players* and *559 Damascus,* both of which were published with scant editorial input and even scantier promotional muscle by the short-lived New Bedford Press. He has also written for the screen, where his credits include the chilling camp classic *Angel Dust: The Whack Attack* and *Disco 9000*.

For all that, it's fair to say that Jefferson is just another example of a black author who has struggled against a publishing world that doesn't give a damn, that is unless its got an affirming message, a likable protagonist, and screams "commercial" in capital letters. But that hasn't stopped Jefferson. Every year he steals away to the Bahamas for a month of serious relaxation and even more serious writing. By the time these words reach you, Jefferson hopes to have finished his latest book, *White Coat Fever,* which he describes as "a drama about unrequited love set against the backdrop of the black medical profession."

Will Jefferson finally be able to quit his day job? Too soon to say. But as you take a few hours out of your busy schedule to enjoy this big bad book, bear in mind that you haven't heard the last from this Old School vet.

FOREWORD

SINCE THE END of slavery black America has lived with the constant fear of imminent annihilation at the hands of an angry white populace unwilling or unable to abandon the legacy of racism. And whether this belief is real or imagined is not as important as the fact it is held not just by members of the African-American underclass, but by America's black scholars and political leaders as well as a substantial segment of the black middle class.

Such widespread support for the perception of black genocide is rooted in an American political landscape that has historically mistreated and abused its African-American citizens. From their use as experimental subjects in the infamous Tuskegee Syphilis Study of the 1930s to the current assault on affirmative action. From the unjustified convictions of the "Scottsboro Boys" to the unbelievable acquittal of four white renegade police officers in the Rodney King case. From the FBI's war against the Black Panthers and the police assassination of Fred Hampton to white America's call for a change in the jury system in the wake of the O. J. Simpson verdict.

And finally, there is the startling revelation that the CIA may well have been deeply implicated in the importation, distribution, and sales of "crack" cocaine targeted exclusively for African-American-dominated inner cities as a way of financing the government's support of the Nicaraguan Contras. This kind of wholesale disregard for the rights, privileges, and welfare of African Americans on the part of the government only serves the bigoted interests of those white male-dominated fringe groups like the militias and skinheads who openly concede their agendas include plans for the coming "race war" against black America.

These are the very serious and dangerous issues that form the underlying premise of *The School on 103rd Street*. It is a work of fiction of course. But it would indeed be unfortunate if future historians view it as having foreshadowed the inevitable "final solution" for the "race problem" in America.

Roland S. Jefferson
January 1997

The School on
103rd Street

CHAPTER 1

THE WATTS SUMMER FESTIVAL was two weeks away, Watergate was the only news of interest, and Muhammad Ali was in training for his title fight with George Foreman. Black folks were still being fucked over, shit upon, and kicked in the ass.

It had been raining steadily for the past week in Los Angeles, a welcome change to the sweltering heat that had prevailed the week before. If you lived in Beverly Hills, the rain brought a freshness to the city; it seemed to cleanse and revitalize everything it touched. If you lived in Watts, you didn't notice much difference—except that the sewers never work. The dark gray clouds and damp air that enveloped the city like a veil seemed to permeate everything.

It didn't usually rain this much in August, and if only for that reason, there was a strangeness that hung heavily in the atmosphere. It was Sunday morning, and the air was still moist and cool from the previous night's rain. There weren't many black folks up at seven, and those who were had to be. At that hour of the morning the only reliable activity in Watts was the routine patrol of the Black and White from the 103rd Street Precinct, with its caged windows and helmeted occupants, menacing, provoking, harassing, challenging, and maiming those whom they were charged with protecting and serving.

Buddy Giles and Leon Davenport were en route to a clandestine meeting that morning, its purpose and content still unknown to them. Their route would take them down Wilmington Avenue, across 102nd Street, and over to Beach Street, some five hundred yards opposite Mafundi Institute. From there a large cluster of trees in the middle of a vacant lot, clearly visible but deceptive in size, marked their destination. Public transportation, being unavailable at that hour, necessitated their having to walk, the inclement weather just another adverse element confronting them.

Leon stepped from the still wet sidewalk onto the muddy vacant lot, his hands thrust deep into the pockets of his faded black raincoat. He was tall for his age, his ill-fitting clothes and worn sneakers reflecting both the style and economics of his peers. Buddy was shorter than Leon, stockier, and wore his hair platted under a knit cap. He was dressed similarly to Leon, though it was here that all similarity ended.

Buddy quickened his pace to catch up with Leon. "Mus' be awfully important for a motherfucker to get out of bed in this weather at this time a mornin'!"

Leon didn't respond; instead, he nodded his head to let Buddy know that he agreed. He pulled his coat collar tighter around his neck and looked to see if they were alone. Having satisfied himself of that fact, he commenced to hop mud puddles as he approached them. By this time they were halfway across the lot, the cluster of trees becoming more distinct.

"Don't see no one there! You?" Buddy's voice was muffled by his coat collar.

"I don't see *shit!* Ain't nothin' here but a lot of wet-ass rain. Man, you know what? I don't get up this early to fuck, and this crazy-ass motherfucker wants me to meet him in the middle of nowhere. Ain't this some shit!"

Buddy remained silent.

"I'll tell you one thing, though; that motherfucker don't show up, his motherfuckin' ass is mine for days. Get me out of bed this time a mornin' for some bullshit." Leon pulled his arm across his face, wiping away the moisture that blurred his vision.

"Yeah, well maybe we early, or maybe his ol' lady wouldn't let him out th' house or sumpin'—fuck, I don't know!" Buddy had faith in Jimmie and had known him a long time. He knew that if Jimmie told him to be somewhere or to do something, that it was usually worth it; some pot; a young bitch willing to give up some pussy; a stolen TV they could sell. He wasn't worried about him not showing up.

He turned toward Leon. "If we're early, we'll wait a few minutes. He'll show up."

"You mean, *you'll* wait a few minutes. I ain't waitin' in the rain fo' no nigger this time o' mornin'." Leon was emphatic, and Buddy had no doubt that his patience was wearing thin.

"You have to admit that Jimmie ain't never run no trips on you, so cool it!" Leon didn't respond. He just kept sloshing through the mud toward the clump of trees that lay just ahead of them now. After all, he didn't really have to be doing this. He had spent the night with a fifteen-year-old bitch who was staying with her elderly aunt because her mamma was shacking with some other dude. He had been trying to get next to her for weeks, and when he finally had the chance, he had to get up to this? No way in hell he'd let Jimmie forget if he didn't show up with something worthwhile. He thought to himself, What in God's name could be this important *this* early in the morning?

As they approached the clump of trees, Buddy once again looked back over his shoulder to see if anyone else was there. The streets were still quiet, the sidewalks empty. "Rain sho' does keep niggers inside, even on Sunday."

"Didn't keep Jimmie inside." Leon's voice was cynical. He repeated himself again. "Didn't keep him inside at all, an' this was one mornin' that he didn't need to leave his house!"

Buddy was still looking over his shoulder when he realized what Leon had said. He turned back toward Leon, who by this time had stopped in his tracks. "What's wrong wif you, nigger? One minute you say he ain't gonna show up, and then the next you claim the motherfucker should stay in his house. I sure as hell wish you'd get your shit together—what's wrong?" Sensing that his remarks may have been premature, he turned toward the clump of trees where Leon was staring.

It was then that he saw what had prompted Leon to speak. They were at the edge of the tree cluster, and from where they were standing they had a panoramic view of the entire area. The still, lifeless form that lay between two trees on the far side sent a chill up Buddy's back. "What is it, a dog?" It was a stupid question and he knew it, but it was the only way he could keep from getting sick at the stomach, since he already knew what and who the form was.

"Shit—dog, my ass!" Leon still maintained his supercool, aloof bravado when he talked, but it wasn't quite enough to conceal the fact he was scared. "That motherfucker is *dead!* Someone offed him real good," he said over his shoulder.

"You don't know if he's dead. He might just be asleep!" Buddy's remarks were now sounding ridiculous at this point.

"Oh, nigger, stop actin' a fool and talk some sense! I don't know any nigger dumb 'nuf to sleep in the rain and mud even if his people put him out the house. 'Sides any one of us would have taken him in—shit—at least for a night."

They started across the clearing toward the other side of the tree cluster, cautiously, almost hesitantly, this time ignoring the mud puddles, their eyes fixed on the form that lay sprawled on the ground before them.

By now there was no doubt in Buddy's mind that the corpse was Jimmie's. He was lying face down in the mud, his hands tied behind his back and his mouth covered with tape that had by now come undone because of the rain. Leon knelt down by the body and grabbed the left shoulder, turning the body over on its back.

Jimmie's eyes had been gouged out.

The sight made Buddy vomit. "Oh Jesus Christ, what the fuck did he do for this? Looks like the goddamn Mafia killed him. Whoever th' fuck it was made sure he couldn't tell what he saw. Shit!"

"You think the Crips offed him?" asked Leon, standing up and backing away from the body. "You know, them some bad motherfuckers! Kill you in a minute over nothin' man, over nothin'. Once killed an old lady—yeah, an old black woman walking down the street goin' shoppin' or sumpin'."

Buddy was quick to Jimmie's defense. "Fuck no, nigger. He wasn't into that gang shit. Nigger spent more time out of school than in. Don't know if he knew any of them, much less if they knew him. Hardest thing he ever pushed was a couple o' reefers, you know that!" He said that because he anticipated Leon's next remark would be about the possibility of some drug-related cause.

Leon's bravado was beginning to break. "I'm gettin' the fuck out of here, man, before the pigs come and blame this shit on me. I knew I should've stayed with that bitch instead of comin' down here with you. Shit, I . . ."

Suddenly he grabbed Buddy's arm and forced him down into the mud behind one of the trees. "What th' fuck wrong wif you, nigger?" Buddy crowed.

"Shut up, you dumb ass! Someone's coming; the pigs, maybe." They crouched low and wedged themselves in between two trees that gave them good shelter but still allowed them to see the lot beyond. From their vantage point they could see south to 103rd Street and Wilmington. Only Mafundi blocked their view of the elementary school that was on the other side of Wilmington. They could see part of the playground area and, beyond that, the edge of Jordan Downs projects.

The figure that Leon saw approaching them in the distance was partially obscured by the fence that surrounded the playground. They strained their necks for a better view, but had to wait for him to cross Wilmington and start on to the open lot before he could be seen clearly. "I think it's Damon." Buddy said, sounding quite relieved. Leon was more skeptical, and his silence was an indication that he would believe it when he could see his face clearly. Buddy looked at Leon for validation of his feelings but found only indifference.

It was starting to sprinkle again, but Leon and Buddy were oblivious to it. Their eyes were fixed on the figure that was working his way toward them through the muddy lot. As the figure came closer to them, Leon suddenly stood up.

"It's Damon," he said. "I can tell by that yellow-ass skin o' his." Buddy stood up, nervously kicked his right heel against the stump of a tree to knock the mud loose, and for the first time looked up to see how much it was raining.

"How many niggers did Jimmie tell to be here, man?" Leon asked. The figure was now clearly visible to both Leon and Buddy.

"Hey niggers, what's happ-en-ing?" drawled Damon who extended his right hand for the customary thumb-clasping handshake that is expected when two black people meet. "Niggers up this early either chasin' pussy, selling dope, or got put out—which one applies to you dudes?"

Damon was a loud-ass kid, and Buddy knew why. His fair skin and light, sand-colored hair were the constant source of teasing and, sometimes, the source of ass kicking. It was necessary for Damon to be loud so as to show other brothers that he was as black as they were. Leon wasn't impressed.

"Stop all that loud-ass talking this time o' mornin', motherfucker."

Before Damon could respond, Buddy grabbed him by the back of his raincoat and pulled him toward the trees where the body lay. He stared at the corpse before speaking. "Damn, what this shit? Who is it—Jimmie?"

"Naw, man, it's Moms Mabley's aunt! Who th' fuck you think it is?" Leon was irritated now and anxious to leave.

"Shit! Who did him in? The Crips? Piru? Bounty Hunters? Kiss my ass, goddamn motherfucker is dead! Shit!"

"Don' know," Buddy answered. "Nigger gangs don't go to no extremes like this jes' to kill a motherfucker—'sides they'd be bragging about it all over town an' shit."

"Well, if they did, we'll hear about it later today," Leon added. It was raining much harder now, and the skimpy raincoats they wore offered little protection. " 'Sides, I don't want to be nowhere near here when the shit hits the fan—dig it?" He pulled his coat collar tighter around his neck and stepped out from between the trees where they were all standing and headed out across the lot toward Mafundi. Without looking back he shouted, "Later, dudes." As he crossed the mud-soaked ground he thought to himself about how Jimmie might have died, about how it must have felt when you know you are going to die and you are helpless to do anything about it. The combination of rain and wind made him lose his balance once or twice before he reached the sidewalk, and by then his only thought was how long it would take him to get back to the house and the fifteen-year-old bitch who was waiting for him in her bed.

Buddy and Damon watched momentarily as Leon departed their midst and sloshed through the mud toward the sidewalk. "Ya know,

I think we best do the same thing, man," Damon said in a cool, quiet manner, quite unlike his usual loud self. Buddy picked up on it but made no comment because he was scared shitless, too. He had no desire to get mixed up in a murder but felt that he owed something to Jimmie, although he didn't know quite what.

"Well, we ought to call somebody, an ambulance or his ol' lady or—"

He hesitated and Damon knew what he was going to say, so he said it for him: "Or the pigs!"

"Yeah, well, somebody—shit! We gotta do something. I mean, we can't just leave him here and forget he ever existed." Buddy was pacing around in the mud as he talked, very agitated. "I mean, I know we can't just wait around for someone to show up, but goddamn, at least we could get him into a morgue or somethin'! I mean, after all!" He looked Damon directly in the eyes expecting agreement, but got nothing. He looked away in disgust and continued to pace around in the mud, putting his hands in his coat pockets at first, then wiping the rain from his eyes.

As he continued to pace, Damon sat down, haunched on his heels, and stared quietly at the body. His right hand cupped his mouth, and his forefinger twitched nervously at the mustache that was starting to appear. Jimmie had talked to him yesterday afternoon and told him about the meeting at the tree cluster. He wouldn't say why he wanted to meet there; he said only that it was very important, something big, something that would affect a lot of people in Watts. It was unusual talk, especially for a kid who was only fifteen! His mind racing now, he tried to think of all the things that he and Jimmie had talked about in the past.

It was about bitches, mostly. Jimmy was bitch crazy, and like most other black kids his age, he began to believe the myth about blacks being sexually superior to whites; being sexual animals. He used to brag continually to Damon how many young bitches he could screw in a weekend. He couldn't imagine Jimmie getting himself killed over a whore! No, it had to be something else; something he knew about and shouldn't; something like dope—yeah, maybe that was it! Maybe Jimmie was going to get into drug traffic.

No, that wasn't like him either. Maybe it was the gang war.

L.A. had it pretty bad in the schools, and niggers were killing each other for petty shit; anything to justify ripping someone off. But he never mentioned anything about being involved in the gangs. And if a nigger intended to rob you, he sure as hell wasn't going to spend a lot of time talking; he'd just kill you and get the hell out of there.

Damon was so engrossed in his thoughts that he didn't hear Buddy call him the first time.

"Hey, dude!" Buddy yelled a second time, shaking him by the collar of his coat. "C'mon, let's go."

"Right!"

"Figure we go over to Mafundi and call someone. Fire department, maybe."

"Yeah, fire department," Damon replied, not really listening, his mind still turning over thoughts about the reason for Jimmie's death.

"You tell his mother? I mean, you know, the family an' all that, OK?" Buddy wasn't asking—he was pleading.

"Let's get out of this fucking rain first before we tell anybody."

"Dig it!"

They were soaked through and through, but it didn't really matter. The lot was nothing but mud now, and there was no such thing as avoiding the puddles. The tree cluster behind them, they walked silently together through the slush toward Mafundi. Damon turned to get one last look, but the trees kept their secret.

"Wonder what Leon is doin' now?" said Buddy in an almost inaudible voice, trying to conceal his feelings. "Probably fucking!" he answered himself, half-laughing, half-cynically. "Motherfucker don't give a shit about nothin', no one!"

The intensity of the rain all but obscured the tree cluster now, and the wind whipped at their faces as they leaned into its force to keep their balance. To Buddy, it seemed like it would take forever to reach the sidewalk. He wondered how anyone could ever be a marine and live this way. He wondered why the hell it rained so goddamn hard in the middle of the summer. He wondered why Jimmie had wanted to meet with him at such an early hour and what it was he wanted to tell him. After all, he was only fifteen.

Why would anyone want to kill a fifteen-year-old kid? Fifteen years old!

As many niggers as there were in Watts, why the hell kill Jimmie? He sure as hell hadn't done the dirt that some niggers did. Damn; just fifteen years old!

CHAPTER 2

Y THE TIME they reached Mafundi they were covered with mud and half out of breath. They approached the building from the rear and walked around to the entrance on the Wilmington side. To anyone not familiar with the community and its structures, Mafundi appeared like just another building, somewhat unusual in design, its light brown stucco color now beginning to fade after years of use. What stood out most of all was the brightly colored mosaic that covered the entire side of the building facing Wilmington Avenue.

The mural was designed and executed by black artists of the community as testimony to their skills that could be learned within. In addition to fine arts, classes were offered in drama, voice, dance, film-making, and radio broadcasting. In recent months, due to the popularity of the center, an antigang group, Brothers Unlimited, had established headquarters there to serve what had become a dire community need.

Looking to the west up 103rd Street, one could see the Watts Writers Workshop, or what remained of it. It was pretty much a mess now. Marquee had never been fixed, there were holes in the brick walls, and the ticket window resembled a carnival. It was being used as a movie theater now, its original occupants having been displaced to a smaller building about a mile or so to the east on Central Avenue and 103rd Street near the park. To the south in the distance stood the Watts Towers, tall pillars made from junk, which now are not only a landmark but also house a small artist colony.

The presence of institutions dedicated to the arts were the direct result of the Watts disturbances of 1965. The arts flourished immediately after the disturbances and city officials, private, patronizing benefactors, and community groups were highly motivated to support this creative seed. But that was all gone now. The remnants were nothing more than curiosities and empty structures whose spirits at one time were the very essence of Watts.

Buddy and Damon didn't give a damn about history when they knocked at the door of Mafundi. They were nine and ten, respectfully, when the disturbances occurred, and lived in other states at that! The intensity and concentration the artists must have gone through when they painted the mosaic meant nothing to them, and not just because they were wet and cold. They reflected the feelings of isolation and despair that settled over the black communities in the seventies, when the realization came that they were hopelessly trapped in a system that perpetuated the status quo.

"Open the motherfuckin' door—shit!" yelled Damon, shivering, his hands thrust deep into the pockets of his raincoat. "Ain't this some shit? Goddamn son of a bitch is lying out in the fucking mud dead, and ain't nobody here yet—shit!"

"I thought sure someone would be here this time o' mornin', but I guess not." Buddy hovered under the narrow transom that was above the door and continued to kick his heels against the concrete in an effort to make his shoes more recognizable. He had no success.

"C'mon. No sense fuckin' with this place. The Service Center is jes' down the street, and . . . !"

"Shit, that motherfucker is probably closed, too," Damon interrupted sarcastically. And then, "Wait! Maybe Carter's there. He's a cool dude."

"Who th' fuck is Carter?" Buddy asked, his face twisting and grimacing at the discomfort the rain was causing him.

"Elwin Carter; Dr. Carter! He's one of the docs at the Center. Got my mom a job there last year. He don't come on like the rest of them bourgeois motherfuckers that work there. We ought ta rap with him about what we found in the lot; maybe he got some ideas."

Buddy remained silent for a moment. "Yeah, well let's go on over to the Shell station and make the call. They got a pay phone outside."

They headed out across the parking lot toward the Shell station, which was on the southeast corner of 103rd and Wilmington, directly across from the 102nd Street Elementary School. They walked past the pumps and over to a small, eggshell-like stand that housed the telephone.

"Gimme a dime," Buddy snapped.

"Shit, poor as I am nigger! Ain't you got no bread?"

"Jes' gimme a goddamn dime, nigger, an' quit all th' bullshit."

Damon reached into his pants pocket, pulled out some small change, and extended his open palm to Buddy. He grabbed at all the coins in his hand, which caused Damon to quickly withdraw his arm.

"Just a dime, nigger! You don't need no more than that."

Buddy smiled sheepishly and took the dime that Damon handed him and placed it in the coin box. The noise created by the sound of the rain upon the eggshell covering made it difficult to hear, and Buddy had to cover his left ear in order to have a conversation with the operator. "Yes, operator, would you connect me with the fire department on 103rd Street?" He paused and turned toward Damon as he waited to be connected.

"Bitches sure take their time!"

"Yes, is this the fire department? Well I want to report a dead body in a vacant lot jes' behind Mafundi. What? Yes, that's right. In a vacant lot . . . what? No, I'm just a passer-by. Don't want no part of it. Jes' thought you ought ta know 'bout it so you could send an ambulance or sumpin'. What? Yeah, sure, bitch!" Buddy snapped as he slammed down the receiver.

"Would you tell me what number you are calling from?" Buddy spoke in a feminine and sarcastic voice as he tried to mimic the manner of the operator. "Ignorant ass bitch! She think I don't know she trying to trace the call. Shit."

"Let's go on down to the Center'n see if Carter is there," said Damon, nodding his head toward the street.

"Yeah, anything to get out of this motherfuckin' rain."

They left the Shell station and crossed 103rd Street, walking east toward the school. A chain-link fence completely surrounded the school grounds, including the classrooms, except for one building that faced 103rd Street at the corner of Grape Avenue. It was a new school; that is, the buildings were new, but the playground was the same; the equipment was sparse, and what was there was antiquated. Each window had a neatly placed burglar bar, which gave the school the appearance of a prison.

Next to the school and farther down on the same street was the Service Center, a series of trailers molded together, giving the appearance of a single building. With the exception of the entrance facing 103rd Street, there were no windows. The school and the Service Center stood together as symbolic evidence of what Watts was all about. They were institutions in a community that had no access to them: a school where knowledge was kept out by indifferent teachers, and by children who knew before they ever started school that knowledge would not make them free; a health center demanded by the community as the result of the Watts disturbances, built from trailors with no windows as if to emphasize the intention of it being a temporary thing—something to keep the black folks pacified.

Like Mafundi, the Service Center had started with much community enthusiasm and participation right after 1965, but that, too, was gone. It had become a commercial venture now, a part of big business that was controlled by the government.

By the time they reached the emergency entrance to the center, they could hear the sirens in the distance. Damon paused at the door before opening it. Looking in the direction of the school, which blocked his view beyond, he commented to Buddy, "Looks like your call got through all right. 'Bout time—shit."

Damon was almost knocked down as the door suddenly swung open and two men and a woman rushed out, opening their umbrellas as they started down the ramp toward the street.

"Sorry, brother," one of the men commented to Damon. "You alright?"

"Yeah, everything's cool," he replied. "C'mon, man," he said, motioning to Buddy as he moved through the door to the inside of the building. The door opened directly to the waiting area, a long hallway with metal chairs lined up against the wall. At the end of the hallway sat a security guard, his chair propped up against the wall on the rear legs.

The chairs that lined the wall were full of humanity and suffering, all waiting their turn to see the doctor. Most had been there for quite a while, sleeping off a drunk. The cry of a child punctuated the otherwise quiet hallway, as a young mother attempted to silence her infant with a bottle. The odor of alcohol was thick in the air, cut only by the pungent aroma of paraldehyde, Septisol, and the stench of vomit. In one corner of the hallway an orderly was beginning to clean up the blood on the floor that had been left by the seven o'clock shift. Damon approached the desk next to the security guard.

"Is Dr. Carter here?"

The guard, still looking straight ahead and smoking a cigarette, remained silent, but pointed with his hand toward the end of another hallway where there was a desk and several women in green uniforms were milling around. He motioned for Buddy, who was still standing by the door, to follow him.

The young black woman seated at the desk was resplendent in her green uniform and cap. Her short-cropped natural and gold earrings gave her an elegant appearance. As they approached her desk, she looked up smiling, sincere, and warm.

"May I help you?"

"Yeah. Look here, is Carter here?"

"You mean Dr. Carter?"

"Yeah, tha's right."

"Well, yes he is, but he's with a patient now. Is there something I can do for you?"

"Not really. I jes' want to speak with Carter a minute, tha's all."

"Are you a patient of his?" she replied quietly.

"No, I jes' want to talk to him. He knows me—tell him Damon

Wilson is here. I'm a friend of his." Damon was talking faster now, his words spilling out in panic.

Sensing the urgency in his voice, she excused herself and disappeared behind the double doors that flanked the desk. She returned shortly and seated herself behind the desk before she spoke.

"He will be with you shortly, Mr. Wilson. Won't you please be seated? There is a coat rack behind you."

"Thanks," said Damon as he and Buddy commenced to make themselves comfortable in two of the chairs that were beside the desk.

After a few minutes passed the young woman noticed that they had not removed their raincoats, and, observing that Buddy was shaking, suggested they remove their wet coats and hang them on the rack. They declined, stating only that they did not plan to stay long. Ten minutes passed before the double doors opened and Carter emerged into the hallway. He was a man in his late thirties, graying in his neatly cut, well-kept natural, and stocky in build. He wore surgical greens with beads around his neck, and a natural comb handle protruded from the right hip pocket of his Levi's.

Buddy regarded Carter suspiciously at first. He had seen black doctors before, but they were usually dressed in shirt and tie or a long white coat. He had never seen any wear beads. There was something about Carter he couldn't put his finger on, something different in his appearance. He soon found out.

"Niggers," Carter said, holding out his right hand to be slapped.

They responded, Damon first, then Buddy. "This here's Buddy, one of my partners."

"Righteous," said Carter, grasping Buddy's hand firmly and securely. His smile was warm and comforting, and Buddy sensed what Damon already knew—that Carter was for real.

"Might help if you took off your raincoats, men." Carter had a way of telling people things by asking them. The message got through. His voice was authoritative but not demanding. His manner was calm, and they felt relaxed in his presence. They hung up their coats and followed him through the double doors into the treatment area. They walked past the booths with the drawn curtains and turned down another walkway lined with empty stretchers.

Carter's office was at the end of the walkway, next to the bathroom. It was a dumpy office, largely because Carter preferred it that way. A single desk cluttered with papers and magazines, old issues of *Ebony* and *Jet* mostly, plus a couple of chairs.

"Sit down, men. Cigarettes?" Carter asked, offering his pack of Viceroys to them.

"Yeah, I think I will," said Buddy. Damon motioned negatively with his left hand and remained silent.

"You know smoking isn't good for your health at all," Carter said as he flipped the match into the ash tray.

"Tell me all about it," Buddy retorted, having difficulty getting the match lit. "Mom said a motherfucker died from a heart attack at thirty and never smoked a day in his life."

"Yeah, well it happens like that sometimes." Carter settled comfortably into his recliner behind the desk and propped his feet up onto the edge. He seemed confident, sure of himself but not arrogant. He pulled out his comb and began to fork his natural with precision.

"Got to keep up my profile, you know. Up kind of early aren't you? You cats plan to be to church on time this morning for sure," he said half-laughing. But before he finished his sentence he knew they had not come to signify.

"We found a dude dead this mornin', over by Mafundi near the trees. Hands tied behind his back, eyes all cut up 'n shit. Made me sick!" Buddy pressed out the half-smoked cigarette in the ash tray as he talked. "We were supposed to meet him in the lot this mornin'—Damon, Leon 'n me."

"Any ideas why he got killed?" said Carter, taking his feet off of the desk. He leaned forward, placing his elbows on the desk, clasping his hands, and resting his chin on his knuckles.

"Might of been what he wanted to tell us about; the Crips could have done him in. . . ."

"Maybe it had to do with dope or sumpin' like that," said Damon, interrupting Buddy. "Even a robbery. Who knows!"

Carter was listening intently as they talked, watching their eye movements and facial expressions. They had his undivided attention, and he watched every movement, every shift in body position, and heard every cough. They told him how Jimmie had called each one of them the previous night requesting the meeting that morning. He had not revealed why he wanted to see them, just that it was important. He only told them that they had to be there, *somehow*. He had not mentioned that the others were contacted when he called them. It was obvious he wanted to avoid their talking with each other. It was all so mysterious. It just didn't make any sense!

"You tell anyone else about this?" Carter asked.

"Called the fire department from a pay phone 'cross the street at the Shell station jes' before coming here. Bitch tried to trace the call and get me involved—shit!"

"Did you . . . ?"

"Naw, I dumped her before she could get a fix. Heard the sirens jes' before we came in, so I guess she put it through; stupid-ass bitch."

"Did anybody see you guys in the lot this morning?" Carter asked anxiously.

"Doubt it! Can't see nothin' from them trees normally, and for sure can't see when it rains like it is now."

"Who else knew you were supposed to be at the lot? Your folks?"

"Naw," replied Buddy. "They knew I left the pad, but don't know where I went."

"Same here," said Damon, nodding his head in agreement. "I leave when I want. Don't know about Leon, though. He's pretty cool. Don't tell people his business."

They continued to talk at length with Carter about what could have been the motive behind Jimmie's death. He questioned them about every move they made, every word they said, who they talked with, and especially about their relationship with Jimmie.

Did they think there was any possibility of his being involved in drug traffic? Had he had any fights at school recently? Anyone been antagonized by him? Had he made a play for someone else's chick? Gotten someone pregnant? His eyes searched theirs for some indication, some clue that might help clear up the mystery. He tended to agree with their feeling that it was not a local situation, but something bigger. Jimmie obviously knew something he shouldn't, but he waited too late to tell anyone who could help him.

There were other thoughts that crossed Carter's mind as he sat listening to their story. How did his assassins know he was going to be where he was at the time? If they knew that, did they also know who he was supposed to meet? Would they be next on the list? He thought it best not to alarm them with his own thoughts, but continued to listen. He was good at that.

The more Buddy and Damon talked, the more anxious they became, and Carter sensed it. He could hear the fear in their voices and sense the uncertainty they felt. He wondered if they had been seen and identified by someone. Would they be questioned by the cops?

He was afraid his face would give away his feelings for them. He did not want to panic them, so he frequently changed positions in his chair, very casually, spontaneously, occasionally forking his natural. He would inject humorous remarks at times to break the intensity of the conversation.

For a moment it was quiet, Carter not having any questions to ask, his visitors volunteering nothing. The silence was broken by a knock at the door which brought Carter quickly to his feet. He leaned across the desk and pushed open the door with his hand.

"Yes?" he snapped, his brow furrowed at the irritation of the interruption. A young orderly appeared and advised Carter that there was an emergency. Carter questioned him briefly about the nature of the emergency, ordered an X-ray, and excused himself.

"You want us to wait here?" asked Buddy as Carter started up the walkway.

"Yes, please. I'll just be a moment. Go across the hall and get some coffee from the machine." He tossed Buddy a quarter and disappeared around the corner.

It took Carter fifteen minutes to take care of the patient and arrange a disposition. When he returned to his office, Damon was deep into an *Ebony* and Buddy was asleep on the floor, his back propped up against the wall. For the first time they noticed the sound of the rain on the roof above them, like the constant roll of a drum announcing the entrance of a king or preceding the playing of the national anthem at a football game . . . or an execution.

"I'll run you guys home just as soon as my relief arrives, which shouldn't be too long from now," said Carter, settling himself once again into the recliner behind the desk. He turned on a small transistor radio he kept in his desk drawer and fished for the local soul station. Having no success, he placed the radio back in the drawer and lit another cigarette. They spent the next few minutes talking about things in general—the upcoming festival, the Freedom Classic with Grambling College, Muhammad Ali's upcoming fight with George Foreman, and USC's chances to go to the Rose Bowl.

Another knock at the door interrupted their conversation, and Carter, raising his voice only slightly, asked who was there.

"Rossmore," came the reply. "Your relief."

"Oh, hey man, come in." Rossmore was young, white, and very proper.

"Ross, meet Buddy and Damon, friends of mine." They did not shake hands, but acknowledged each other verbally.

"Did you leave me anything?"

"Just one lady in congestive failure. I've started her on Digoxin already, and they're getting a chest film now. Rest of the patients are waiting to go to County."

"Hey, that's swell, Carter," said Rossmore in his usual liberal patronizing way. "I might even be able to get some sleep before all the Sunday morning garbage comes in." Carter bristled; he restrained himself from hitting Rossmore by opening and closing his desk drawer, as if looking for something. If it had been in a hospital somewhere in Beverly Hills, Rossmore would have said patients; but in the ghetto patients were garbage, something to be discarded.

Carter tried to reason with himself: Rossmore thinks he's doing black folks a favor, coming down here to work. After all, he considers himself a liberal in the true sense of the word. He would never be able to convince him otherwise. If he called him a racist, even if he could explain to him the meaning behind his comment, it would probably go over his head!

Carter didn't bother. He slipped off his green top and put on his dashiki that had been hanging behind the door, grabbed his umbrella and motioned for Buddy and Damon to follow.

"See you tomorrow, Carter," said Rossmore grinning "Glad to have met you b . . ." He coughed in an attempt to conceal his mistake, but it was too late. Damon finished the sentence for him.

"Boys, honky!" he said contemptuously.

"Look, I really didn't mean . . ."

"Kiss my ass, you white motherfucker." Damon was motionless, staring at Rossmore coldly, waiting for him to say the least thing that would provoke him.

"He's new, Damon. He'll get an education about black folks soon enough," said Carter, trying to hide the frown on his face. He grabbed Damon firmly by the arm and headed down the walkway, Damon reluctant but yielding.

Carter left some last-minute instructions with the nurses at the desk in the hallway before heading toward the exit. Buddy was waiting by the door, Damon having already gone outside to let the rain soothe his anger. They huddled together under Carter's small umbrella and walked down the ramp toward the street.

"Where you parked?" asked Buddy.

"Down the block near the fence."

"You park on this street! Man, ain't you 'fraid your ride will get ripped off?" Buddy asked.

"Yeah, well, if they want it that bad, I can't stop them. I've been lucky so far I guess."

They reached Carter's blue VW parked near the end of the block.

"Oh, I see why now," said Buddy laughing. "Not the most sought-after 'chine in the world."

"Really," chimed Damon.

Once under way, Carter punched the buttons on his radio, looking for the soul station. When he heard spirituals come through the speakers, he cut it off. "I forgot it was Sunday. Had my share of churchgoing and all that!"

"Turn to 105, Doc," said Buddy from the back seat. "I can dig some jazz."

"Can't. Don't have an FM."

They rode through Jordan Downs projects, turned onto 103rd, and headed west. Buddy lived in the same project that Damon lived in, Nickerson Gardens. It wasn't far from the Center, but in the rain the drive would take them ten minutes. They rode the entire distance in silence. The only noise was the constant squeak of the windshield wipers on the glass and the drone of the motor as Carter went through the gears. Carter cracked his window slightly as he lit a cigarette, and the moist air quickly cleared the fog that was beginning to form on the windshield.

Nickerson Gardens was like any other project in Watts, with two-story frame and stucco buildings with four to eight apartments per building. There were some fifty to sixty buildings in this complex, clustered together like army barracks. Most were poorly painted, with well-worn paths leading through sparse patches of grass to the sidewalks. Windows that had not been replaced were covered with blankets or had been boarded up with plywood. The rain made the few patches of grass appear greener and washed the sidewalks of their silt. In the streets were parked cars, bumper to bumper, hogs to sportscars, trucks to motorcycles.

"You can let us off here, Carter," said Damon, breaking the silence.

"Right."

"Tell your mom I said hello." He snapped a quick clenched fist at them, which they returned. As they headed down the sidewalk to the projects, Carter rolled down his window and watched them until they disappeared into the maze of buildings. He continued to stare out the window as if hypnotized until a horn behind him broke his preoccupation. He drove off, winding up the window in the process, and headed toward the Harbor Freeway. He wondered if they knew the value of their ability to survive. What would become of them in a few years? They were so young, yet the future offered them nothing but despair and mistrust. They were locked in with nothing to motivate them, nothing to stimulate their abilities. In his preoccupation, he passed the freeway and had to make a U turn under the bridge in order to get back to the entrance. He turned onto the northbound ramp of the freeway and entered the flow of traffic. Once again thoughts flooded his mind.

There ought to be something he could do to help Buddy and Damon; some way to insure them a chance at surviving. He thought about Rossmore's smart-ass remark. He was too brainwashed to even realize the meaning of what he said, much less to be able to correct it! Well, maybe there would be something he could come up with to help, something that might let him get involved in their lives in a positive way.

CHAPTER 3

THE *LOS ANGELES SENTINEL* headlined Jimmie's death as the result of "gang violence." After all, that was the most logical explanation.

L.A. was swept up in a *wave* of teen-age gang violence, mostly black gangs fighting each other; disrupting classes, assaulting teachers, extorting younger kids, and, in some cases, forcing the schools to shut down altogether. For some reason nobody could make the connection between the decline of the Panthers, the BSU, and the Black Congress, and the general increase in black gang activity in the city. "Investigative journalism" was nonexistent in the black community, so there was no motivation to question the reason behind the death of any black person. Jimmie became another statistic, another death, considered the result of "black on black" crime in the ghetto.

Carter folded the paper under his arm, sipped his coffee slowly, and stared quietly out of the window of his plush Baldwin Hills home. The funeral was at ten that morning, and he had made plans to attend the service. He had spoken to Damon only once since the incident and had agreed to ride with him and his mother in the procession. Neither Buddy nor Damon had seen or heard from Leon.

Carter rinsed out his cup, walked to the den, and turned on the stereo. The soft, muffled voice of Al Green filtered through the speaker system: "*Have you been making out OK?*" Carter turned up the volume, adjusted the treble, and headed for the shower.

It took him thirty minutes to shower, shave, and dress. He didn't like funerals and was reluctant to attend this one, doing so only at the insistence of Damon's mother. It was nine-thirty, and Carter compulsively checked each door to make sure that it was locked.

Many of the homes in Carter's neighborhood had been broken into more than once, necessitating the installation of burglar bars on the doors and windows. No matter how decorative they were, to him they still resembled bars on a jail, and he was reluctant to create that effect on his pad. His home was cantilevered out over a drop, making access all but impossible except through the front entrance. In most instances, the robbers were well-organized groups of professional thieves. All those apprehended were black. All too often Carter was reminded that his affluence subjected him to a different kind of oppression, and to a host of problems that he shared with his neighbors.

Being black was no security, and he agonized over his thoughts that it was not worth it to accumulate things because of the constant fear that they would be taken away. He enjoyed his home and his neighborhood, which was all-black, the whites having moved out gradually over the past ten years, selling their homes at inflated prices to blacks who, all too often, mortgaged their souls to demonstrate to the world that they had made it. His neighbor to the right was a postal employee whose wife had to work to insure that they could meet the monthly note, which was three times the amount of the average check of a welfare recipient. His neighbor to the left, a hustler, was seldom home in the evenings and drove a new Rolls Royce every year that he reportedly had paid for in cash. Across the street lived a young schoolteacher, a divorcee, who augmented her salary with child-support payments to insure that the bank would not foreclose on her.

Having satisfied himself that everything was in order, he went to the garage and began to pull the cover off of his Italian sportscar when he caught himself. This is no social occasion, thought Carter. Besides, it would be too pretentious. He replaced the cover slowly, being careful not to bend the radio antenna on the right side. "That's alright, precious. See you later this evenin'," he said aloud. He had given himself thirty minutes to get to the funeral home, but that was predicated on driving his Ferrari. Having to take the VW meant that he would be late.

He was.

The soloist was singing by the time Carter arrived. He took a seat in the back row and, when the services were concluded, moved to the parking lot adjacent to the chapel to wait for Damon and his mother. They soon joined him, along with Buddy.

"Got room for one more?" said Buddy.

"No problem."

"Now Dr. Carter, you *know* I can't ride real comfortable in that little car of yours. Can we go in mine? I'll drive." Mrs. Wilson's voice was hoarse as she spoke. She was an obese woman of forty, pleasant enough but somewhat overbearing.

"Be my guest," Carter said smiling. He knew what was really behind her desire to take her car, a recently purchased used Eldorado. She lived in the projects and augmented her welfare check with a small salary she received as an employee of the Service Center. She would probably lose the car in the next six months, but during that time she would demonstrate her affluence, even if there was no food in the house. A twinge of guilt came over Carter as he walked toward the green Eldorado. She had wanted to show off, and hadn't he wanted to do the same? He examined his own motivations; after all, it was important for her to let people know she was *somebody,* even if her values were misguided. He wasn't too sure that his were any better.

The procession wound snakelike through the streets of Watts en route to the cemetery. They passed from one project to another, from corner liquor store to corner liquor store, past vacant lots, boarded-up buildings, and single-pump gas stations. Epithets effaced almost every building and, although profane, revealed the prevailing sense of frustration, despair, pain, and rage: "Long live Mark Essex"; "Support your Black Liberation Army"; "Off the Pigs"; "Malcolm X Forever"; "Freedom Now."

The burial ceremony was brief but well attended. Carter noticed that there were even some whites in attendance, probably from Jimmie's school. The noonday sun in all its brightness couldn't eliminate the stench of this blighted ghetto. Carter walked briskly back to Mrs. Wilson's Cadillac only to find that the air-conditioning unit was nonoperative. His patience wearing thin, he loosened his tie, removed his coat, and motioned for the rest to hurry up. The cemetery was adjacent to a garbage dump, and with the slightest breeze the smell became nauseating. The combination of the heat and odors made it almost unbearable. He paced beside the car, wiping his forehead and neck with his silk handkerchief, while Mrs. Wilson seemed to talk with everyone she saw. Sensing his irritation, she apologized for the delay and headed the car in the direction of the cemetery gate.

Carter, seated up front next to Mrs. Wilson, engaged Buddy and Damon in conversation whenever she wasn't talking. Damon smiled at Carter when he turned around on occasion, knowing that his mother had an endless stream of chatter that was irritating and tiresome. It wasn't until they were well under way that Carter noticed the constant presence of the blue Ford LTD some five to ten car lengths behind them. Trying not to act concerned, but wanting to confirm his suspicion, he asked Damon's mother to turn at the next signal, under the pretense that he knew a shorter way to beat the traffic. She obliged by turning west onto El Segundo Boulevard.

In the distance he could see the LTD make the turn, although he couldn't make out the occupants. His constant stare out the back window alerted Buddy and Damon to the fact that something was wrong.

"What is it, Carter?" Buddy asked, looking first at him and then out of the window.

"Not sure. I think we're being followed."

"Followed? By who?" Buddy's voice revealed apprehension.

"Mrs. Wilson, turn right at the first street past Ujima Village, but keep the same speed." They repeated the turns three additional times, the LTD keeping its distance.

"Maybe they goin' the same place we goin'," she said.

"Not hardly, Mrs. Wilson," Carter replied.

"Well, what you want me to do now? I mean, I don' want to get in no trouble!" She was frightened, and so, to quiet her anxiety, he suggested that she drive straight to the funeral home by way of 103rd Street, since that would take them right by the precinct on 103rd and Compton Avenue.

As they approached the police station, Carter asked her to slow down but not to stop, regardless of the LTD's position. He wanted the LTD to get close enough so he could see the occupants or get the license number, but Mrs. Wilson brought the Eldorado to an abrupt halt directly in front of the police station and frantically began blowing the horn. As the traffic began to back up behind them, Carter saw the LTD make a turn onto Compton Avenue and disappear. Then he had to physically restrain Mrs. Wilson from blowing on the horn and reassure her that they were no longer being followed before she would continue. During the commotion one or two cops observed them from the station but made no effort to intervene.

Less apprehensive, but still frightened, Mrs. Wilson drove on to the funeral parlor. She was concerned about what to do if it should happen again. She tried to get some reassurance from Carter, but he had none to offer. He wasn't even sure they were being followed, much less what it might mean.

It was Wednesday, and, as everybody knows, doctors don't work on Wednesday. Carter was no exception. They chatted briefly in the parking lot about the events of that morning. Mrs. Wilson invited him to dinner. He declined, saying that he had other plans for that evening, but that he would take her up on it at another time. Damon was to keep in touch. He would.

It took Carter forty minutes to get to the Playboy Club in Century

City. Almost without exception, every Wednesday at noon he had lunch with a group of his colleagues at the Playboy Club buffet. Recently after lunch he had been spending the balance of the afternoon and early evening driving the Ferrari up and down Pacific Coast Highway; not to style, but because his love for cars had a special meaning to him. It was his way of relaxing, of finding peace within himself. But today he was going sailing. Calvin had invited a group aboard his thirty-foot Coronado, which he kept in a slip in Marina Del Rey.

To his surprise, Carter was the third one to arrive. Calvin, of course, had been there for some time. He was nattily attired in white bells and a blue-and-white striped turtleneck sweater that was obviously too small for him. His captain's hat sat awkwardly on top of his full natural, and his black skin stood out in stark contrast to his outfit. His loud and coarse laughter would be annoying to all except those who knew him intimately.

"Carter, baby! My main man, what's to it? You bring your bad-ass machine with you?" He held out the palms of his hands for Carter to slap and then gestured for him to sit down. "Nigger with that monster has got to have all the bitches in the world—shit!"

"Not me, man, I just want ta be like you, ya know, with a yacht an' all that. Hell, there ain't no doubt in my mind that the bitches *line up* for a piece of you." He smiled and offered Calvin a Kool.

Calvin was an egotistical and obnoxious son of a bitch. He bragged continually about how many white women he had at any one time. If he mentioned it once, he mentioned it a thousand times. As a surgeon his skills were marginal, but he never let one forget that he had trained at the finest "white" institution in the country.

"I made a hundred grand and didn't pay no taxes!" he would say repeatedly. He lived at the Marina in a fifteen-hundred-dollar-a-month apartment and drove a Mark IV. "White on white, in white" was his favorite expression. Despite all the arrogance about him, he took up sailing on a dare and became quite good at it, but his prime motivation, once he realized that he had the skill, was to be able to "style for the brothers" and let niggers know that he had made it.

Today would be his day.

"Will the real Superfly please stand up?" Carter said, extending his hand across the table where Simon Kupp was seated. Kupp, a pediatrician, was very fair, with straight hair. He was a Meharry graduate from Louisiana who had come west after his internship. He had opted not to go into private practice but was more academically inclined, though his grades never demonstrated that, and accepted a teaching position at one of the local medical schools. Kupp was quiet except when he was drinking, and that was nearly always. Carter always teased him about his drinking, saying that he would be dead in four years. Kupp would be dead in *less* than four years.

"Where'd a nigger get a name like Simon Kupp? You ought to be a Jew or something," said Calvin, sipping his drink. "Besides, what the fuck reason you fool with niggers anyway—shit! Man, if I looked as good as you, I wouldn't go nowhere near niggers! I'd become invisible! Like Flip Wilson says: 'Hoo-ray for the invisible,' " he added, jerking his head and snapping his fingers in caricature.

"Kupp ain't got the problem 'bout being black that you do," said Carter, sipping the martini the Bunny had just brought him. "Anyway, nothing wrong with the way you look. It's strictly a state of mind."

"Bullshit, man; you mean to tell me if I looked like Kupp I wouldn't have it made? Don't try to shit me! Kupp, you could be *free* if you passed. Don't that mean *anything* to you? I mean, after all, man, you could have a big Beverly Hills practice taking care of all the rich white folks' kids an' all that. The banks wouldn't hassle you; you could borrow as much as you want, when you want. I don't understand you, man! You choose to identify with black folks knowing that you could really pass for white? I don't *understand* that shit!"

Kupp smiled, stirred his drink slowly, and leaned back against the seat.

"Carter, would you tell the man he is sick, please?"

"Calvin, you're sick."

"Yeah, yeah, yeah, don't tell me, let me guess. You're gonna tell me that your skin would be free, but your *mind* would still be in bondage. Don't bother. I've heard it a thousand times!"

"That's very good, Calvin," said Kupp cynically. "You have a good memory. I like that in a man. We only discuss this every week!"

"Hang in there, Calvin baby," Carter said, slapping Calvin's back. "We'll let you be invisible." Calvin remained silent and shook his head from side to side in disgust. The Bunny asked if they wanted more drinks. Only Kupp ordered.

"Where the hell are the rest of the niggers—shit! I want to eat and get the hell out of here and get with it." Calvin was impatient, and as he spoke he saw three figures walking toward the table.

"Goddamn! It's about time! Ain't nothin' like bein' on time. You folks sure believe in C.P. time, don't you?"

"Gentlemen of the black bourgeoisie, I salute you," said the tallest of the three.

"Hey Chris, what's to it, man?" said Carter, standing and shaking his hand. "Dr. Christopher Ramp, I presume. Haven't seen you in three or four weeks. Where the hell you been keeping yourself?"

"Been on vacation. Carter, you know Parson and Scott, don't you?"

"Right. What's to it?" he replied, acknowledging them. They seated themselves at the adjacent table and ordered drinks.

Chris Ramp was a gifted internist. Graduating at the top of his class from Howard, he did his graduate training at the University of Texas and then took a fellowship in endocrinology at Stanford. He was a doctor's doctor, and his colleagues knew it. His personality left much to be desired, however. He was sarcastic with his colleagues as well as with his patients, and his personal life had been a disaster. He had been married and divorced four times in the past ten years, and although it was never proved, it was rumored he was homosexual.

Bobby Parson was an obstetrician and a financial success. To him, medicine was a game, but his real love was money. He was unscrupulous, unorthodox, and unethical, and he had no apologies for being so. He made most of his money doing abortions for wealthy white clients before the pill became popular. Wise investing in questionable projects pyramided his fortune to the point that he was able to take a year off from his practice and still had a taxable income of $100,000. He had a villa in Montego Bay, Jamaica, and a condominium on the Costa Del Sol. You knew he was a millionaire because he told you so. With the exception of the group at lunch, he had few friends and no professional respect. He could care less.

Casey Scott was a trip and a half. He studied medicine because his mother wanted him to. He took up radiology because it was a nine-to-five gig with no night calls, but everyone knew that radiology didn't pay Casey's bills. He was a gambler and had been since his early days at Meharry. As a poker player he was superb. He was able to quit his job as a lab technician while in medical school and support himself on his winnings. Once in practice, his routine seldom varied. Tuesday and Thursday evenings he played poker in Gardena. Friday night through Sunday you could find him in Las Vegas. Recently he was considering giving up the practice of medicine altogether and enrolling in law school. He was married to a white woman who had two kids from a previous marriage. They seldom entertained, mostly because Casey was ashamed of her appearance, since she was obese and rather homely looking. Despite the fact that he kept mostly to himself, Casey could be counted upon to give you the shirt off his back if it was necessary. Nobody ever had anything unkind or bad to say about him. He was just one of the guys. That was the way he liked it.

Cecil Menlow joined the group midway through lunch. He was called Angel by his colleagues because of his good looks. Not particularly bright, he was from New Jersey and had a middle-class background. A lot of pressure had been placed on him to study medicine. Uncertain as to what he really wanted to do when he finished school, he drifted around the country, going from one residency to another until he settled in Los Angeles. He was single and had a lot of women and a bachelor apartment in Hollywood. He wound up in general practice in a neighborhood that was mixed and had office hours from eight to twelve every day but Sunday. He made it a point to associate himself with the theatrical set and could hold an audience spellbound with tales of the private lives of various black entertainers. He drove a leased Rolls Royce with license plates that spelled ANGEL.

"Angel baby, the man with all the women," Calvin shouted across the room. "Do you see that suit the nigger is wearing?" he said, referring to the Edwardian-cut outfit. "And look at the motherfucker's shoes—jes' like stilts. My man is clean today."

"I'm clean every day, Calvin. You should take a lesson from me; I could get you straight, man."

"Now ain't this some shit. Do you hear this nigger talking! Angel, how the fuck you gonna go sailing in that outfit? I told you to wear something casual and tennis shoes if you have 'em!"

"That's what I wanted to drop by and tell you. Can't make it today. Suppose' to be up at Bill's pad at two-thirty this afternoon. You know, Bill and I been friends for some time, and he wanted me to drop by. I'll catch you when you go out again, though."

Kupp, grinning broadly, couldn't miss the opportunity. "Why, you told me last week that you were suppose' to meet him this week. How come you tell us you been friends for such a long time? You got to be the biggest bullshitter in the motherfucking world."

The group broke out in loud laughter at Kupp's remark.

"Shh . . . you fools—white people are looking at us," said Angel.

"Fuck white people!" said Ramp. "Fuck all white people!" he repeated, only this time much louder, while holding up his glass and looking around.

"Cool it, Ramp," said Carter, grabbing his forearm and forcing it down. "Let's eat so we can move out and get on my man's yacht."

Ramp looked at Carter contemptuously but complied. "You know something, Carter," he said, "it's niggers like that who make it bad for other black folks, know what I mean? Why should he be concerned about what honkies think of him—shit. They ain't concerned about what niggers think! Shit, all he's concerned about is his goddamn image with the white folks."

"Hey, yeah, I hear you!" exclaimed Carter. "But I guess that's his problem."

"How long you stay in the war, man, twenty years? How the fuck could you work around honkies that long, huh?"

"I couldn't!" Carter replied. "That's why I got out after twelve. Shit start goin' down funky for the brothers when the Nam thing warmed up, an' hey, I was an officer and it was bad for me—shit—so you know what it must have been like for the younger dudes."

"Army? Navy?" asked Ramp, more subdued now.

"Force."

"Yeah, well, I can dig it," said Ramp, downing the last of his drink.

"No way in hell they ever get me to stay longer than the two I gave 'em, doctor or no doctor. Fuck *that* noise!"

"Look here, Carter, you still going with that little chick you told us about last month, the one whose old man died?" Parson added.

"You mean Sable? Oh, yeah!" he exclaimed smiling.

Calvin, having overheard the question, quipped, "That is one *fine* sister. Carter, my man, you got good taste, for days!"

Carter broke out in a wide smile, folded his napkin on the table, and lit a cigarette. "I'll show you how to do it sometime."

"Will you *listen* to this nigger talk his trash! Ain't this some shit!" Calvin reached up and grabbed Carter by the neck, pretending to strangle him. "This is what I should do to you," he said, laughing as he slowly shook Carter's head from side to side.

Carter, gesturing with his cigarette towards Calvin, directed his comment to Parson, who was seated directly across the table from him. "You know this fella, man? He's a buddy of yours, isn't he? You sure keep strange company."

Parson, his mouth full of food, shrugged his shoulders, shook his head, and managed an intelligible response. "I ain't never seen him before in my life. *Definitely* not a friend of mine."

They were all laughing now, cracking jokes with each other and enjoying one another's company. Their conversation seldom changed from one week to the next, yet it was therapeutic, to say the least. During a lull in the conversation Carter let himself drift in his own thoughts. Sable would be back today. It had been three weeks since he had felt the warmth of her body next to his, or seen the seductiveness in her smile. This was the longest they had been apart since they started living together eight months ago.

During her absence he had the house carpeted in lush shag,

45

refurnished the bedroom, and purchased a Ferrari Dino. The first he expected would please her; the second didn't matter—the car was for him. There was a strangeness about her that worried him. She seemed unsettled, was constantly on the go, usually attending a meeting or a conference on civil rights. Her husband had died of a heart attack at forty-two, leaving her well insured. Since there were no children, she was the only beneficiary and her monthly check made her financially secure.

She came and went as she pleased. That was the first thing she told him when they met: "I really dig you, but I have to do my own thing," she said. He accepted the relationship for what it was and had no regrets. When they were together, they would spend hours talking, making love, and enjoying each other. When she was gone she would call daily, and they would talk for five minutes. She would mail him trinkets, nothing expensive, but always something that would please him—a key fob, a tie, a tie clip—and once she sent him a pair of sunglasses with horn rims. He had to have the lens refitted, since they were not prescription, but she never found out.

Calvin's loud mouth evaporated his daydream. "Like the man says, 'Let's get it on!'"

"Hey, hey, hey," yelled Scott from the adjoining booth. "Move out. Let's get the show on the road."

"I'm gonna give you niggers some culture today, show you how the white lord and master lives. We is going yachting, gentlemen," said Calvin facetiously, tilting his captain's hat back on his head.

"Yes indeed, I'm gonna teach *all* you niggers how to sail. I even got some Dramamine so you don't have to get seasick!"

"Jesus, how long do we have to listen to this?" said Kupp, shaking his head.

"I always said, you give a nigger a little education and some money and he'll *always* act a fool! Now who ever heard of a nigger on a sailing yacht before? Niggers are suppose' to own power boats, not sailboats, 'cause that takes *brains*. Why you know they got white boys who haven't even finished high school that know how to sail? Hey Calvin! They ever let you in the Yacht Club at the Marina?"

46

"Kiss my ass, Casey. I ain't into no social scene, man. This is purely esthetic."

Casey looked at Carter and feigned a cough to keep his laughter from exploding.

They spent the afternoon on Calvin's boat. It was clear and the wind was ideal. Despite the fact that none had been on a boat before, they enjoyed themselves. Kupp became seasick despite the Dramamine.

Although Carter found himself relaxed, he was preoccupied with the thought of seeing Sable again. There was so much about her that he didn't understand.

CHAPTER 4

THEY RETURNED TO THE MARINA at six, leaving Carter approximately two hours before Sable was due to return. He would not have to pick her up at the airport because she always left her car in the long term lot adjacent to the airline terminal. He drove to the Crenshaw Shopping Center and grabbed a quick meal at Sugar's.

Fifteen years ago Baldwin Hills, View Park, and Baldwin Vista were lily-white, and a black person, any black person, would have been unable to purchase a home or rent an apartment in what is now affectionately known as the Jungle. Like a cesspool, the shopping center spreads out below the hills in a fan shape, its conduits bursting with masses eager to spend their money on products they neither own nor produce, but only consume. Now Crenshaw was black; its businesses geared to the black life-style. Store leases changed as frequently as traffic signals, and, where display windows once went unchallenged, they have been cemented over, creating a monolithic and faceless facade of concrete and steel.

He purchased a pair of patent-leather platform shoes by Rossi for sixty-five dollars at Richard's Shoes and then stepped next door to Charlie's Men's Shop and ordered a green suit with red stitching on the lapels and a pair of Fred Astaires, all by Petrocelli. A gold turtleneck sweater by Michelangelo and a pair of gabardine socks to match were added. He spent the remaining time window shopping in Santa Barbara Square, adjacent to the Crenshaw center, where he thought he might find something for Sable. He was unsuccessful.

Driving back home, he pondered his own environment. Carter knew that the only difference between the Crenshaw district and Watts were the external accoutrements; otherwise, it was still a ghetto with its inhabitants paying exorbitant rents to absentee land-lords who lived in Beverly Hills. There was constant intimidation from the police, its children were subjected to gang terrorism, its welfare recipients were subject to continued harassment because they chose to live somewhere other than Watts. There was job discrimination, social discrimination, religious discrimination, health discrimination—all the things that keep black people enslaved were painfully evident to Carter as he drove slowly down Santa Rosalia toward Stocker Street. The seduction of affluence was glaringly demonstrated as he observed a young man regally dressed in full Superfly garb arguing with a gas station attendant about the price of new tires on his recently purchased, used Mercedes 250.

He passed the high-rise medical building on Santa Rosalia with its office space fully leased year after year to black physicians by its white owners in Hollywood. Though never confirmed, it was rumored that the building had been paid for three times over by its present occupants. There had been talk of developing a group to buy the million-dollar marble monument, but each time the plans fell through because of someone concerned that someone else would get more, and all the while its occupants still paid their rent to the man in Hollywood.

His thoughts about the Jungle were fleeting as he headed up Stocker Street, and by the time he reached Hillcrest they were gone, to return again only when he ventured off the hill. The bland smell of oil filtered through Carter's window as he approached the crest of Stocker and turned north on La Brea. The oil wells were silently, slowly, monoto-nously masturbating the earth of its essence, their fields surrounded by chain-link fences and traversed by high-tension wires.

Before he reached Don Milagro Drive he knew Sable was already home. She had caught an earlier flight from Dallas and arrived some two hours ahead of schedule. She greeted him affectionately, nibbling at his ear, whispering, caressing—his response no less than hers—the static between them more intense than that caused by the newly laid shag. She was an attractive woman of thirty-four, her close-cropped natural adding a touch of elegance to her high cheekbones and rich brown hue. Her light green eyes presented a striking contrast and always drew attention to the unusual combination. She was short, and since she was in the habit of going braless, the fullness of her breasts was convincingly outlined by the jersey sweater that seemed to cling as though it was painted on her.

She drew herself closer to Carter, burying her head in his neck and slowly rubbing her ankle against his calf. "You miss me, baby? Huh-"

"What do *you* think, mamma?" he replied, his hands gently caressing her buttocks. "I think I better sit down. You know what you doin' to me."

"Hmm, is that a fact?" Sable responded in an almost inaudible whisper. Smiling, she continued her seduction, her tongue seeking his in mutual consummation. His hand filled with the firmness of her breasts as she groaned her approval. He opened his mouth to speak, but she placed her fingers across his lips, preventing any sound.

"Shhh, don't talk now, just enjoy. Got plenty of time for talk later." The moisture from her skin blended harmoniously with Carter's, and she enjoyed the feel of his stubble across her cheek.

"When did you get the carpet laid?" she asked softly.

"Last week," came his forced reply.

"That means I'm next," she giggled, as she thrust her hand into his crotch. She waited for him to pick her up, his strong arms enveloping her like a cradle. He would take her into the bedroom, where they would spend the rest of the evening. He was as predictable as a clock, and she loved him for it because he brought order into her life where there had only been chaos.

Morning came abruptly, the sun's rays rudely interrupting the darkness of the room as it forced itself in through the curtains.

Sable stirred first, negotiating the sheet that entwined them like a cocoon. It was clear, and from the bedroom window the view of the city was spectacular. She opened the curtains, exposing the full width of the window, flooding the room with sunlight. Carter rolled in his sleep, the warmth of the bed beside him now cool, the darkness now yielding to light. For a moment Sable said nothing, staring down at the form that lay before her. How nice it would be to have him home with her all day today, her first day back.

That was out of the question.

She knew Carter as few others, and the one thing he seldom did was avoid his responsibility to his patients. She drew the belt to her robe around her waist and, as she left the room, pulled the sheets completely off Carter. He would be awake within the next ten minutes. She was in the midst of cooking breakfast when he entered the kitchen, yawning and stretching. Grabbing Sable from behind, he kissed her neck and fondled her breasts gently.

"You really are a titty freak, you know. You should see a doctor—I'm serious. I don't know *what* I'm going to do with you." Her eyes were closed, and she was smiling as she talked. "You best let me finish your breakfast, man. Are you hungry?"

"Nope, I'm full."

"Full?"

"Yeah, ate all I could last night!"

"You sure are a nasty nigger."

"Ain't I though? You know, honey, you sure did it to me last night."

Sable smiled and winked. "Got a hard day, baby?"

"What's today? Thursday? Yeah—shit—sickle cell clinic today. Whole lotta sick folks due in today." Then he said, "Hey look, we didn't get much chance to talk last night. How did the meetings go?"

"You did a lot of talking last night," said Sable, smiling sheepishly.

"You got any complaints about my conversation?"

"No indeed! Cream or sugar?"

"Both!"

"The meetings went as well as expected," Sable finally answered him. "Honkies really did a job with the money, though. Niggers don't get shit. Hey look, you realize how whitey has fucked with our minds? Man, it's a trip! He's got niggers killing niggers, and not just on the street either. We do it to each other on the political level, too. Play those silly-ass games just to get some bread! Butter your toast before it gets cold. I think they're going to have to file a class-action suit to break open the Busing issue."

"When do you have to go again?" Carter asked, running his hand up and down her thigh as she dished out his eggs.

She backed away playfully. "Don't you ever get enough, nigger?"

"So when do you have to go back?" Carter repeated himself, somewhat irritated. He hoped it would not be at least for another month or two.

She surprised him. "Not until after the first of the year." A broad grin broke out on her face as she awaited Carter's response. It was predictable.

"No shit! That's outta sight, baby. Hey, look here, we gonna really get down then," said Carter, now smiling euphorically.

She seated herself across the table from him and watched him eat. She seldom ate breakfast herself, usually preferring only two meals a day. She lit a cigarette, holding the match stem until she could feel the heat of the flame as it burned toward her fingers. She sat silently as the smoke rose upward in single columns like long-stemmed roses, disappearing against the ceiling.

She had never smoked before her husband's death, and then only when she became nervous. His death left her shattered. An emotional wreck, she sought solace by involvement in the movement, such as it was, where she could be around people and stave off the feelings of isolation and loneliness that crept over her like a plague. She would become so depressed at times that she would find herself sobbing uncontrollably, the pain of despair eating away at her like maggots, which remove all substance from their victims, leaving nothing.

She had met Carter in Washington, D.C., not quite one year after her husband's death. He was attending the National Medical

Association's annual convention, and she was a delegate to the quarterly meeting of the National Black Social Workers. They met at a social that was sponsored jointly by the two groups. She had liked him from the very start but did not expect to hear from him after the meetings. She was living in New Orleans at the time, and he called, asking her to come to California. She did and decided to stay.

She had no reason to regret her decision.

Carter did not interfere in her private affairs. She had learned to trust him, and, although it was difficult to do, it became the first step toward returning to her old self. He had offered to accompany her in the beginning, but she preferred to go alone.

He did not press the issue.

"You been in the garage yet?" he asked.

"You mean since I've been back?" He nodded affirmatively, finishing the last of his coffee.

"No. Why?"

"Got myself a new toy while you were gone."

"Oh, I see," she said matter-of-factly.

Carter had anticipated her lack of response, but he would show her the car regardless. Taking her by the hand, he led her into the garage through the entrance that adjoined the kitchen. She folded her arms across her chest and stood quietly staring as he peeled off the car cover. She circled the Ferrari slowly, saying nothing while she peered at the reflection on the hood. Bending over and squinting to make out the chrome insignia on the fender, she tried her best to appear interested.

"Body by who?"

"Pininfarina! It's a Ferrari, Sable, a *Dino*. Do about 150 mph *all* day long." Her lack of interest more obvious than he anticipated, he replaced the car cover and motioned for her to go inside. He would take her for a ride later that evening if she wanted to go, but it didn't really matter. He would go alone.

"Be careful with that thing, OK, baby?" Sable's voice was sincere. She knew what exotic cars meant to Carter, but try though she may, she couldn't bring herself to like them. High speed bothered her, and he drove fast every chance he had, something that made her feel uneasy when they were together.

"You better get dressed. Oh, and turn on the stereo on your way to the bedroom. You driving today?"

"No, Mathis's turn today. What's your schedule like?" The sound of the Jazz Crusaders filled the speakers, Carter having to reduce the volume in order to hear her response.

"Very loose. I had hoped you'd be around, but since you can't I might go out and register for school." Sable approached Carter, who was standing in front of the speakers, put her arms around his waist, and entwined her leg with his. "Dance with me."

"I thought I had to get dressed!" he quipped.

"One minute won't hurt, baby." They danced in half-time to "So Far Away," the thick shag massaging their feet as they moved from side to side. When the tune stopped they silently stepped apart, Carter departing for the bedroom where he would dress and Sable to the kitchen where the dishes awaited her touch. They would take her seven minutes, and she would return to the bedroom to watch Carter finish dressing. Sable was seated on the edge of the bed, her legs crossed, the front of her robe falling to one side, exposing the upper part of her thigh. Its rich brown color provided an almost iridescent effect against the blue, green, and gold quilt upon which she was resting. Carter was in front of her admiring the shine he had just given to his shoes. She wanted to reach out and touch him, but she resisted, her emptiness satiated for the moment. She was curious.

"How did you happen to choose green, honey?"

"Green?" He regarded her puzzled, searching her eyes for a clue to her question, but they revealed nothing.

"The rug, *dummy!*"

"Oh yeah. Well, I knew that green was your favorite color—outside of black, of course—and so I had the man find me a green shag that I thought you'd like. Was I right?"

"You always are!" she exclaimed, provocatively wetting her lips with her tongue.

"What do you think about the furniture I got for the bedroom?"

"Well, you really haven't given me much of a chance to look at it since I've been back, but I would say it's satisfactory," she said, smiling in a seductive manner. "Especially the bed, for *days!*"

"Really is! Hey, baby let's have a party this Saturday night! We'll celebrate your return, have wall-to-wall niggers, an' all that, OK?"

"Doesn't give us much time to get ready!"

"Hell, ain't nothing to *get* ready!" Carter exclaimed. "I can buy the 45s, and each nigger can bring his own booze. I know who to contact to get some grass—shit—baby, we'll have us a *good* time, yeah. *'I'm gonna take you high-er . . . '"* Carter sang along with the tune by Sly that blasted from the speakers, snapping his fingers to the beat.

"Shall I make some snacks, dips, or whatever? You know how niggers love to eat! I can get Janice to help out. Besides, she'd *love* to meet some dudes that got money."

"Sure, if you want to go to all that trouble, baby, but we just having niggers over. No sense in going hog wild! Niggers can have a good time with just the *bare* essentials." He winked at her as she jumped up on her feet, pulling her robe tightly around her, and walked briskly through the door into the living room.

"You sure are nasty."

He followed behind her, forking his natural with his right hand, his left slapping her on the buttocks as she tried to skip away from him.

At that moment a car horn sounded in the driveway. Carter slipped on his coat and grabbed his bag, opening it to make sure that everything was where it was supposed to be.

"Where is my otoscope?"

"Your what-scope?"

"My oto—never mind, I know where it is." He disappeared into the bedroom, and returned momentarily, the otoscope in his left hand. "I forgot that I charged the battery last night.

"Later, baby, see you tonight. You want to go out for dinner, the Marina maybe?"

"Why not?" She kissed him firmly and convincingly, her large breasts pressed up against his chest. He tapped her once again on the buttocks and moved for the door.

He entered the light blue Chevelle parked in the driveway and waved as the car disappeared down the street. Sable closed the door, secured the latch, and walked over to the stereo. She switched from FM to phono and put on a record by the Fifth Dimension. As the melodic and graceful sound of "Stone Soul Picnic" filled the room, she picked up the phone and dialed Janice.

"Hello, Janice? Sable. Yeah, I got back yesterday. Well, you know, the first day is for my old man. Right! Hey listen, you want to help me with a party we're going to have Saturday night? Huh, oh yes, honey, Carter says *we* are gonna get down for *days*. Lord *yes,* niggers galore! You got your choice—all sizes, shapes, and colors. I think people will remember this one." She finished her conversation with Janice and settled into the recliner that faced the stereo. She glanced at her watch: 11:45 A.M., the dial still set to Eastern Standard Time. The fatigue of the three-hour time difference still hung over her, and she found herself yawning repeatedly in its wake.

She noticed a strange silence about the house despite the music, its draped windows and acoustic ceilings reflecting a chamberlike atmosphere. She allowed her body to go limp in the recliner, the music becoming a distant echo as her mind drifted into the obscure. Her last thought was about the party. Perhaps it was a good idea at that. It might bring some excitement and energy into her life.

CHAPTER 5

DREXEL MATHIS LIVED in an apartment in the Jungle, worked as a drug counselor at a local drug rehabilitation center, and supplemented his income by selling grass to white kids in Hollywood. He didn't like either job but had no choice. Twice decorated, twice wounded in Vietnam, he had been given a dishonorable discharge for a minor infraction that had racial overtones. He was brilliant and industrious but had no funds for school, and the discharge kept him from gainful employment in all but the most humiliating positions.

Carter was responsible for getting him on as a counselor, but they had made a deal: no grass to black kids, just whitey! Mathis agreed and kept his word. They had also agreed that he would stop pushing altogether if Carter could get him into industry. Carter had spent six months trying to convince employers that his military background had no relationship to his abilities. His plea fell on deaf ears. He wrote letters, arranged interviews, and aptitute tests, and even coached him on the kinds of responses he should give. Up to now he had had no success, but today he had an idea that might just work.

"Sorry I'm late, man, but I had a drop to make. Today sickle cell day?" Mathis asked, after finally pulling up to their meeting place.

"Every day is sickle cell day, my man," Carter responded, getting into Mathis's car. "You gotta be cool with that shit, Mathis. The man don't play!" He was concerned that Mathis would get busted before he could get into something legitimate.

Perhaps he had promised too much.

He knew that Mathis was bright, but that didn't stop his feeling of uneasiness. A narcotics rap would put the lid on the box, and Mathis would never get out.

"Hey look, I gotta idea that might work this time. You ever have any kind of physical ailment in the war?" he asked.

Mathis was silent for more than a minute before he answered, the sound of his car's worn-out muffler permeating the interim.

"Yeah, yeah, Doc, I did. I was in the hospital for a week because of bronchial trouble. I don't remember what they called it, but it wasn't pneumonia."

Carter began to fish. "Bronchitis? Bronchiolitis? Emphysema? Bronchiectasis? Anything like that?"

"Don't know, Doc. Them white boys don't ever tell you anything."

"Yeah, dig it. Well, look here, let me tell you what I got in mind." He explained to Mathis that there were funds for training in industry through the Department of Rehabilitation, for persons who have some form of permanent disability. He proposed to declare Mathis such a case, thus making him eligible. It would take some manipulating, but he thought he knew whom to go to to get it together. He would need his army records for a start, so Mathis would have to sign a release.

He wanted to encourage him but cautioned him not to be overly optimistic. They would have to run a game on the system, but with the bureaucratic machinery so cumbersome and the naïveté of the officials, it just might work. They would be unlikely to scrutinize a carefully prepared report of a physician. With any kind of luck he would be in school within sixty to ninety days.

"Hey look, Doc, if this shit works, I owe you. Anything, man, just anything. You're a pretty regular dude, man. Sure wish the rest of the brothers were like you."

"Oh, there's a lot of us around—just never been asked, that's all."

"Yeah, but nodody had to *ask* you, man, you just got your shit together. I really dig that." Mathis stopped abruptly at the crosswalk to let the kids pass on their way to the 103rd Street School. "Kinda reminds me of when I was in school. Of course, that was in the South, and we only went half-day 'cause we was in the fields the rest of the time. *Damn!* I wish I could have finished!" He pursed his lips and that look came over his face of a person who had been taken to the well but not allowed to drink from it. Carter sensed his frustration and tried to neutralize it.

"Well, hey, don't let it get you down, man. You got too much on the ball! You ain't gonna be down forever. Next stop is mine, buddy. See you at five—no, wait! I gotta meeting this afternoon over at King. I'll catch a ride from there. Later!—Oh, and come by around lunchtime so you can sign a release, OK?"

"Right on, baby! Later."

Carter was fifteen minutes late, a bit unusual for him, but he would make it up in the afternoon. The rain had stopped, and Sable was back.

It would be a good day.

He had that feeling of expectation, of anticipation, about him, and it radiated to those he came in contact with. His whistle, his walk, everything about him said that he was feeling good. He was.

His office was as he had left it—a mess. He quickly changed clothes and went to the emergency room, where the sickle cell clinic was in progress. His first patient was his most difficult: a nine-year-old black girl brought in by ambulance. She appeared lethargic, weak, and above all, pale—something many white physicians missed when treating black patients. Carter pressed the child's thumbnail and watched for the pink color to return. It didn't. Her skin was dry, and her respirations were shallow and labored. The nurse reported a temperature of 103 degrees. The child's mother repeated the history to Carter as she had a thousand times before on each episode that brought the girl to medical attention.

She was born with the disease and had spent a good portion of her young life in hospitals. The mother had done her best to protect the child from the elements, since they were always a constant threat and might throw her into a crisis. The rain over the past week didn't help. She had caught a cold, and the nightmare and the agony started all over again. She usually had pain in her legs and arms, but this time it was different. She lost her appetite, had no strength and no desire to play. She knew the treatment regimen by heart: fluids, Demerol for pain, bed rest, and antibiotics for infection. She knew the terminology, though not necessarily the meaning: SC disease, SS disease, hemoglobin electrophoresis, and thrombotic crisis.

"Call pediatrics and get me someone over here, and get X-ray and lab on the phone, *stat!* We got a sick kid on our hands."

Carter reached for a bottle of Ringer's lactate, hesitated a moment, and then exchanged it for five percent dextrose and water.

"Tourniquet and intracath, please, with an 18-gauge needle."

Carter tied the elastic band around the girl's upper arm and massaged her fingers in an open-and-closed-fist manner until the veins began to appear one at a time. He removed the plastic covering from the needle and brought it close to the girl's skin, simultaneously palpitating the vein to make certain that his needle would not miss its mark.

Satisfied of its location and size, he pushed the needle through the black skin and into the void below. Holding his breath, he continued to direct the needle toward the vein by feeling its movement under the skin. Suddenly the catheter attached to the needle filled with blood, and Carter removed the elastic band and motioned for a piece of tape to secure the needle. He then cautiously began to thread the slim plastic catheter through the needle and into the vein. His young patient grimaced with discomfort, but was too weak to effect a physical response. The catheter met no resistance and, when fully extended, Carter removed the needle and placed a piece of gauze under the tip to prevent its accidentally puncturing the skin during its use. He taped the needle and catheter firmly to the skin and requested the nurse to secure her hand with an arm board to minimize movement. He opened the clamp to the tube that connected the dextrose and water and watched it flow into the catheter, the blood returning to the vein as quickly as it had appeared.

The pediatrician arrived, discussed Carter's findings and procedures, and examined the girl again.

"She really looks pale. Better get her typed and crossmatched for three units of blood. I'm willing to bet the peripheral smear shows an aplastic crisis in which case she'll have to be transfused. What did the chest film show?"

"Not back yet, but she's probably got junk in her lungs. Chest sounds terrible. Moist *rales* in both bases."

"I hope it's not a staph pneumonia, 'cause if it is she . . ."

"X-ray is ready, doctors." The cute nurse directed them to the viewing box adjacent to the nurses' station. They studied the film for a moment and then conversed.

She was lucky.

It was simple bronchial pneumonia, and though both lung fields were involved, it was easily treatable with antibiotics, positive pressure, and a croup tent. Whether or not to transfuse would be based on the results of the smear. A call to the lab confirmed the pediatrician's suspicions: hemoglobin 3gm percent, white-cell count twenty thousand, and the absence of any reticulocytes on the smear. Red cells were 1.65 million.

The child's mother was seated in the waiting room next to the treatment area. Her head bowed, she sobbed quietly to herself. Carter joined her and explained the findings, but she didn't hear him. Wrapped in her own thoughts, she was full of guilt and self-doubt. Why had she brought this child into the world with such a handicap?

Carter didn't understand her anger.

"Why me? Why did it have to happen to my child? I didn't do anything to deserve this! My *baby* didn't do anything! It's not fair—it's just not fair! Why don't *their* children have it?" she said, pointing in the direction of others in the waiting room across from her.

"I know how you feel."

"Do you have sickle disease?" she asked bitterly.

"No."

"Then don't tell me you know how I feel, man! You don't know what I have to *go* through with her!"

"It must be very difficult," said Carter softly.

"Damn right it is! I can't do anything because of that child. I'm afraid to go anywhere 'cause she might have an attack. All she does is hold me back. I can't . . ." She buried her face in her hands and wept uncontrollably.

Mathis arrived at Carter's office promptly at noon to sign the release. They had lunch together at Mother's Cafe on 103rd Street of ham hocks, black-eyed peas, and greens—the best in the city. Carter ate there frequently, the small café a polyglot of the community. The jukebox played soul music continuously, and there was always the aroma of fresh-cooked food, born of the Delta but transported to Watts, losing none of its qualities during the journey. Ninety minutes found them outside once again, the sun drifting lazily behind the cirrus clouds until only haze remained. They talked briefly in front of the Service Center as they observed its clients moving through the entranceway. Some in search of medical attention, others in search of attention, and a few, just searching.

Carter attended his team meeting that afternoon as well as the monthly meeting of the medical staff. He was amused at the antics of his colleagues who were there to "serve the community" but whose only reason was a check. He was also gratified by some of the younger physicians who were there because they wanted to be. His lunch having settled comfortably, he dozed throughout much of the meeting, waking only when the discussion centered on vacation time and sick leave.

His rest was interrupted by a phone call from the emergency room. A young woman was comatose. History from reliable relatives revealed that she had taken an excessive amount of tranquilizers an hour or so before as the result of an argument with her husband. Carter left the meeting and arrived in the emergency area as they were preparing the stomach pump. The family could give no information about the type of tranquilizers taken. Her pupils were pinpoint, her pulse thready and weak. She did not respond to pinprick stimulation nor to orbital pressure. Carter estimated her age at twenty. Old scars across her wrists indicated this was not the first time she had attempted to take her life.

"Get an EKG for me, please, and start D5W one thousand cc., wide open! Give me her vitals every two minutes!"

"Blood pressure ninety over fifty; pulse is sixty, weak!" the nurse snapped. Carter placed some KY jelly on the tip of the long rubber tube that was connected to a bulblike structure in the middle. He rotated her head to the side and forced her tongue out of the way as he began to pass the tube down her throat. She gagged only once but otherwise remained still. The nurse wiped the saliva from her chin that was exuding from her mouth and placed gauze patches over her eyes to prevent the corneas from drying and becoming infected. At the two-foot mark Carter stopped the lavage tube, secured it to the side of her face with tape, and placed a plastic airway between her teeth to insure proper ventilation during the lavage procedure.

"You can attach the funnel now," he said to the nurse at the head of the stretcher. He began to gently massage the rubber bulb in the center of the tube until the stomach contents began to fill in the vacuum. Clamping the tube below the bulb, he squeezed it again until the contents were expelled through the end of the funnel and into the bucket on the floor. The funnel was then filled with Normal saline, and the reverse process took place, with the stomach filling to its capacity with saline. They repeated the procedure for several minutes until the dark red color of the stomach contents changed to clear.

"Looks more like 'reds' to me," he said. "How much of the D5W has she had?"

The nurse checked the bottle. "About three hundred cc."

"Give her twenty milligrams of Ritalin IM and start nasal oxygen. How's the blood pressure?"

"One-twenty over seventy, pulse is much stronger. Her respirations are much more regular now, but she still doesn't respond to any stimuli."

"That's all right. Her vital signs are improving. As long as she's ventilating well, she'll do OK. Someone give me a stethoscope!" Carter repositioned the woman on her side and placed the bell of the stethoscope against her lungs, listening for any clue that would indicate a problem.

"She's clear in both fields."

He turned her back over and listened to the heart sounds, slowly moving the stethoscope around the perimeter of her chest.

"Sounds OK."

He wrote some orders for the nursing staff on the ward, adjusted the flow of D5W, and left the emergency area to speak with the family. They were all gone except a young woman about the same age as the patient. When questioned, she became frightened.

"Hey look, Doc, I don't want no trouble. I just know her, that's all!"

"Look, baby, I ain't no cop. But I gotta know what she took so I can treat the woman right, OK? So what did she take?"

Uncertain of herself and even more so of Carter, she remained silent, her eyes oozing with mistrust. She studied Carter's face for a while and then spoke.

"You promise you won't tell her I told you?"

"Right on, sister woman."

"Well, she and her old man had a fight and all that. She told her folks she took some nerve pills, but that's bullshit, 'cause I know better. She had a whole bunch of red devils 'cause we . . . I mean *she,* been dropping for a long time. But look! She ain't no addict! I mean, you know, everyone drop a red now an' then. That's all she took, Doc. She didn't take no tranquilizers! Is she gonna be all right? I mean, she ain't gonna die is she?" Carter reached out and wiped the tears from her cheek, and in a manner and tone that was almost inaudible, reassured her.

"She'll be OK, baby. Thanks for telling me. It was important. I won't tell her, but she owes you one. Don't forget to collect."

"When can I see her?"

"Later today or early tomorrow. When she comes out of it. We got the junk out of her stomach, so all she has to do is sleep it off. Give me your number. I'll have the nurse call you."

She tore off the corner of a DWP envelope, scribbled a number in pencil, and pushed it into his hand. As she turned to go, Carter grabbed her arm and moved in front of her.

"Thanks, thanks a lot," he said softly. "You're good people."

She looked him in the eyes for a split second, her face reflecting an expression like the Mona Lisa, half-smiling, half-crying.

"Yeah, anytime, Doc." She walked slowly toward the exit and disappeared into the daylight.

Carter gave the nurse the piece of paper and returned to his office, where he commenced to open his mail and return his phone calls.

Damon Wilson had called at noon, but when he returned the call, no one answered. He thought of calling Sable but remembered that she would be out at the university. The rest of the day was routine. He lanced an abscess on the leg of a man, removed a splinter from the hand of a child, treated ten cases of flu, and pronounced one man DOA from a gunshot wound of the chest.

Five o'clock didn't come fast enough for Carter. Normally he would be in no rush, but the thought of Sable waiting seemed to slow the hands of the clock to a standstill. He tried Damon's phone once more before leaving but had no success. He had almost forgotten about the meeting at King Hospital when he was reminded by a flyer on his desk.

He caught a ride with another staff physician and arrived on time. As he had anticipated the meeting wouldn't commence until five-thirty. It was the monthly meeting of one of the local black medical societies, its leadership inefficient, socially naïve, and politically impotent. They had long since disgraced the name of the physician who was its founder, the ideology and purpose lost in obscure and meaningless rhetoric.

Its membership was classically divided: conservative against liberal, old against young, and astute against naïve. It was the only black organization in the city that was consistently nonproductive, yet still managed to have its members mentioned in *Jet, Ebony,* and the *Los Angeles Sentinel* as being connected with some worthy cause that, more often than not, came to their attention after the fact.

Their wives entertained in pseudo-social style, the pecking order usually determined by the length of their mink coats, the cost of their homes on the hills, and the color of their Cadillac Eldorados. They gave charity affairs, held Tupperware parties, and acted as volunteers during the Watts Summer Festival. Their boredom was handled by alcoholism, extramarital affairs, and Beverly Hills psychiatrists. Their children attended private schools in the Valley, traveled to Europe in the summer, and came out as debutantes with the Links. They climbed the social ladder as fast as their husbands were audited, the competition no less intense than between players on an athletic field.

Few, if any, of Carter's friends attended the meetings except on special occasions when legitimate issues were to be discussed. Today was not one of them. The meeting was lengthy, boring, and poorly attended. After an hour he left with three others who shared his sentiments, though not necessarily his principles. Traffic was thin at that time, and when they dropped Carter off in front of his house, it was seven o'clock.

Sable was dressed and ready, her light eyes flashing anticipation at the evening ahead. She was anxious, however, and paced the floor continuously while she smoked, waiting for Carter to change.

She had spent the day at school as she had said and signed up for three graduate courses in the Master's program for Black Studies: "Comparative Black Religions," "Theories of Oppression," and "Strengths of Black Families." Although she had a degree in elementary education, she never had taught because she hated the field, having studied it only at the request of her parents, who wanted to insure that she would be a "proper Negro" with nice middle-class strivings. She had fallen for the seduction, but the movement spread to Nashville like a brush fire and she became a part of history.

For the first time she faced the reality of oppression. As a student at Fisk University, secured by the monthly checks from home, she denied to herself that the sit-in demonstrations were relevant, that they had any meaning for her. But she found her classes sparsely attended, her boyfriend never available, and teachers observing her, puzzled at her continued presence on campus in face of the social upheaval downtown. She finally relented when her roommate asked her one evening, "Don't you want to be free?"

She observed first from a distance and gradually became involved until she was so swept up by emotion that she became one of its leaders, her health no longer a concern, her education secondary, and her social life confined to jails and restaurants. She had undergone a profound experience, and it left her bitter and confused. She found herself challenging her values and the values of her parents and discovered they were incongruous and made her uncomfortable. She married a young attorney from Harvard, and, though still uncertain of her direction, she adapted surprisingly well once again to the middle-class facade. His precipitous death reawakened all of the old feelings of anger and disillusionment that she had experienced as a student, throwing her once again into emotional turmoil.

"Hurry up, will you! I'm hungry!" she shouted to Carter through the open bedroom door.

"Only be a minute more, baby. Cool it." As Sable paced the floor she rubbed her arms where scars were the only remnants of once open, festering burns caused by cigarettes that were extinguished by white patrons of the restaurants in Nashville. She paused for a moment, the glowing ashes from her cigarette reminding her of the pain she had endured willingly in her quest for freedom.

They had dinner at Cyrano's in Marina Del Rey and then went to the Name of the Game on Century Boulevard for some dancing. At midnight they went down to the Lighthouse to hear Gabor Zabo, and, on the way home, they dropped by Shelly's Mann Hole and caught the last set by Gerald Wilson. Carter had taken the Ferrari, and, although Sable offered no resistance, she didn't encourage him. From Shelly's they headed down Highland toward Wilshire, Carter keeping the Ferrari in second gear, its four overhead camshafts anxious to unleash its power, the high-pitched whine of the engine drawing provocative stares from others in passing cars. When he reached the freeway, he nudged the sleek black Ferrari into the flow of traffic, but it needed no coaxing, its rapid acceleration and exquisite maneuverability responding obediently to Carter's command. The car reached the speed limit in a matter of seconds, its fish-mouth grill and recessed headlights against a low profile creating a grotesque and gargoylelike appearance as it moved swiftly and unchallenged down the concrete ribbon.

Carter smiled as he settled comfortably into the bucket seat. He pulled at the shoulder strap to insure its security and, as methodically as an airline pilot, regarded each gauge, each switch, each instrument to make certain that there were no malfunctions. Although he had purchased the car only weeks before, he knew it intimately; its low center of gravity, quick steering, and disk brakes took some getting used to, but he was an able student. He considered it a jewel, a functional masterpiece like a Swiss watch—the ultimate combination of design and performance. It looked awkward and out of place among the rectangular and vile products of the Detroit metal factories.

Carter always drove with his left hand on the steering wheel and his right on the gear shift, while he spent as much time regarding the rear-view mirror as he did looking straight ahead. The cops always followed sports cars, especially the expensive, exotic ones from Europe, and particularly if the driver happened to be black.

Sable reached in the glove compartment and pulled out a tape cassette by Hank Crawford and after three minutes returned it, the scream of the engine making it almost impossible to hear.

"You like that, baby?" Carter shouted, the smile still on his face.

"Couldn't hear it. Too much noise!"

"I mean the engine, honey!"

"I guess it's all right. Little loud, isn't it? Is it supposed to make that much noise?" Her face frowned as she regarded him inquisitively.

"That's all a part of it, baby. That's what it's all about. I mean, you have to feel it *in* you." He slowly caressed the leather covering on the steering wheel as he talked. "Shit, baby, this is an animal—it's what cars are supposed to be."

To Sable the noise was monotonous and irritating; to Carter it was hypnotic, a synthesis of man and machine in synchronous action. She would never understand.

It was after two when they arrived home, and, although mindful of the fact that he had to be at the Center by nine, they made love repeatedly until the sun winked at them from around the edges of the closed drapes. As he lay exhausted in Sable's embrace, he gamely fought off the temptation to sleep and reluctantly removed the sheets, now stained and discolored by their mutual consummation. Cold water did not remove the fatigue, and a cup of Maxwell House coffee did little more. He returned to the bedroom to finish dressing, pausing only to run his hands through her hair as she slept soundly in the aftermath of repeated orgasms.

He wrote her a short note and taped it to the door of the refrigerator before he left. Once again he checked his bag and, finding it in order, left the house quietly, being careful not to slam the door lest it awaken Sable. The VW seemed obtuse. To Carter it was as esthetically offensive as the Eldorado, but it got him to work and back and that was all it was supposed to do. His eyes still heavy with sleep, he drove to the Center in a daze. His radio, tuned to the local black station, played the number one and number two soul tunes back to back, but it did little more than just keep him awake. As he passed Will Rogers Park he could see the workmen starting to assemble the booths that would be teeming with people in a few short weeks as the festival once again commemorates the agony that is Watts, its explosions still echoing eight years later.

He was late again, and although it was the exception rather than the rule at the Center, he was concerned that it did not become a habit. He was not a saint, but he did feel that his patients had the right to expect that he be on time when it came to their health care. It would be a difficult day for him, and not just because he had not slept, but because his thoughts would be on Sable. He could feel the anticipation building now for the party tomorrow night. There hadn't been a good house party in the last four months, and folks were ready.

The day went as expected. His routine varied little, except that he didn't go to lunch but locked his office door and slept for a full hour. That evening they would eat at home and catch an early movie at the Gilmore Drive-In. There would be many preparations to take care of on Saturday, and he had to help Sable as much as possible. It would be necessary for him to get some rest tonight, but his desire and affection for her would more than likely prove an obstacle to that end.

As he drove home from the Center, his thoughts centered on his fatigue. He would try and convince her to take a rain check on the movie.

He was sure she would understand.

CHAPTER 6

SABLE HAD SAID the party would begin at nine, but she really didn't expect anyone to show up until ten or eleven. She was right on the money. They began arriving at ten-thirty and continued arriving until two. Carter had stocked the bar the way conservationists stock a lake with trout. There was Johnnie Walker Red, Chivas Regal, Jack Daniel's, imported Nebbiolo Cinzano, Jamaican rum, Tia Maria liqueur, *crème de cacao,* and Beefeater's gin. He bought a generous supply of Seagram's V.O., Courvoisier cognac, Canadian Club whiskey, Akadama red wine, and several cases of Miller High Life.

The first to arrive had no use for Carter's bar.

Nick Bannister was a dentist of somewhat eccentric behavior. He drove a black Mercedes 600E with curtains in the windows and a small bar in the back of the rear passenger seat in which he kept White Mateus, Pink Chablis, and Benedictine and Brandy. He was always aloof in the presence of others, owing to his need to impress people that he was wealthy, when in fact he stayed one step ahead of his creditors. His Mercedes was not equipped with an air conditioner, but he would drive around in the heat of the summer with the windows up in the pretense of having the air conditioner on, so as not to reveal the fact that he was unable to afford the installation fee. He was married to an attractive woman who was equally phony, her claim to fame being a bit part in a recently produced black film of some notoriety. That made her an actress, and she never let you forget it, her conversation centering on little else.

They made it a point to keep in the company of the theatrical set and as a result seldom missed receiving an invitation to black social events. They had anticipated only temporary involvement with the black middle class before rising another notch on the ladder, but in reality they had become permanent fixtures.

Lavender Armstrong came to the party alone.

A tall, angular woman in her late twenties, she had extricated herself from an adolescent marriage and confined her efforts to running her string of beauty salons throughout the black community. A product of mixed parentage and the ghetto, her attractiveness was neutralized by her caustic personality and liberal use of profanity. From an external appearance, she was classically middle class, well dressed and always in the best company. Everyone knew that she was never in the presence of the same man more than once because few men could put up with her castrating personality after meeting her.

Seated at the bar with her half-empty drink, she drew an admiring glance from Kupp, who was standing at the other end. He moved to the empty seat next to her and ordered the bartender to replenish her glass. She placed her finger over the top and shook her head to indicate no. The bartender regarded Kupp for a moment, shrugged his shoulders, and returned the bottle to its place in the rack on the wall.

"Don't you want another drink?" Kupp asked. She continued to sip from the glass, peering at Kupp from over the rim, but remained silent.

"My name is Simon Kupp. I noticed you when you first came in and thought we might get acquainted. You're a sharp-looking woman, and that dress you have on is out of sight!"

"Just because you compliment me doesn't mean you gonna get any pussy, nigger!" Her remark caught him by surprise. He had thought she was bourgeois, a nurse perhaps. He decided to pursue it further.

"I think you got the wrong impression, miss. I just wanted to get to know you." She continued to stare at Kupp across the rim of the glass, her face expressionless. She put the glass on the bar and, in what would be her last comment to him that evening, brought it right down front. "Listen, you yellow-ass motherfucker, niggers like you come dime a dozen! You think that just 'cause you one of them Creole types all bitches supposed to kiss your feet? There're very few niggers that can do anything for me, and you *definitely* ain't one of them! So don't come on like some kind of 'proper Negro' shit with me, OK?"

Kupp took one last sip from his glass and, without responding, left the bar to join the crowd in another part of the house. His ego slightly bruised, he sought out Carter for an explanation of her attitude.

"Man, that bitch is a *crazy* motherfucker—shit! Man, she is *sick!*"

"Who you talking about, Kupp?"

"That fine-ass high yellow bitch at the bar. I tried to hit on her, but she ain't nothin' but a street nigger—shit!"

"You must mean Lavender—tall chick with a curly natural?"

"Yeah."

Carter laughed from behind his glass. "Yeah, well you have to know how to approach her, man. She's a pistol."

"Pistol, my ass. That bitch is *crazy*! But I have to admit, I sure would like a piece of that."

"Well, I understand she's a freak," Carter said.

"Yeah! Well freak on *me*—shit!"

They continued to file into the party at ten-minute intervals, some alone, some in small groups of twos and threes, like animals going into an ark. The black bourgeoisie, a menagerie of pseudo-affluent pocketbooks and plastic minds, would escape for one evening the flood of oppression that threatened to drown them on a moment's notice. They would indulge their fantasies tonight. They felt themselves the chosen ones, the ones that had made it, no matter how precariously.

They would dance to the music that had sustained their forefathers in the cotton fields of Mississippi and Alabama, and was now sustaining them some three hundred years later. For one evening they would try and forget that they were still niggers, still slaves, something they all knew but had to deny in order to preserve their self-esteem. For one evening they would get down, hear James Brown, Al Green, Marvin Gaye. They would talk that talk with each other, shuck and jive, and pretend that freedom existed. In the morning they would have to awaken to the painful reality of survival, but for tonight those thoughts would be immersed in the music and dancing that would occupy their attention.

Janice had arrived early in the evening to help Sable prepare for the party. She was cute but obese and lacked the sophistication to style herself so as to make the best appearance possible. She was a bright person, had an affable personality, and mixed well in all circles. She had been in social work since graduation from college, but recently decided to return to school for her doctorate. She felt frustrated in relationships with men but refused to believe that her obesity had anything to do with her failure. She had had an affair with an older white man who was married and, although she didn't particularly care for him, it was better than no company at all. It ended when he called her a nigger one evening after an argument.

She had insisted that Sable introduce her to all available men that evening, both single and married. Sable obliged, but soon found out that Janice could fend for herself. Her appearance gave her an entrée into conversation with men that proved captivating.

She would catch herself someone this evening for sure.

She did—a young intern from King Hospital who was as thin as she was large. For some reason he found her cute face and large limbs strangely sensuous. Janice wasted no time, her conversation with him becoming more provocative as they talked. He suggested they leave the party for a while and get better acquainted. Like a good social worker, she was accommodating and excused herself to Sable. She returned two hours later quite fatigued but obviously pleased. She and the intern spent the remainder of the evening in the kitchen, which delighted Sable, since this left her free to participate more fully in the party.

Cecil Menlow came to the party with a strikingly attractive woman whose large breasts slowly fluctuated from side to side when she danced. She was an actress who was working her way up in the film industry. Short on talent, she would do whatever was necessary to land a big part, which usually meant landing in the bed of anyone who might have influence enough to get her onto celluloid. Tonight she would be with him because she had heard that he knew the director of a film she wanted to appear in. Short on brains, she had relatively little to say to anyone for the greater part of the evening, except, of course, Angel.

"Would you *look* at the size of those titties!" Kupp whispered to Chris Ramp as she walked past them en route to the bar.

"That bitch needs a goddamn wheelbarrow to keep those things up. My man Angel really has his shit together tonight."

"For days. Jesus, would I like to fuck *that!*"

"Easy, Kupp. Remember, you're a guest tonight. Must act accordingly."

"Shit! Accordingly my *ass!*"

Just at that time Calvin approached Carter from behind and tugged at his coat sleeve.

"You see that bitch Angel brought tonight?"

Carter nodded affirmatively.

"I have to give him ten points. She must be at least a 42-D cup. Course, you can't *tell* anymore since those bitches stopped wearing bras. She must smother that motherfucker to death. Bet he plays telephone every night."

"Why Calvin, I didn't know you were interested in such things. What would your *patients* think of you?" He shook his head in playful disgust as Calvin's eyes followed the plunging neckline as it left the bar.

"Yeah, well they just have to think what they want—shit! Easily a 42-D!" He wheeled around and shook Carter's hand. "Party is out of sight, man. Say, where's the grass? I can smell it but can't tell where it's coming from."

"Men's dressing room out by the pool," he said, pointing in the pool's direction with his glass.

"Right on, Carter baby!" Calvin sauntered across the room and disappeared through the sliding glass doors.

Bobby Parson had come to the party alone. He had forgotten about it until it was too late for him to get a date. The one thing he didn't forget was his two-hundred-dollar pocket calculator by Texas Instruments. Unlike his peers, all of whom owned calculators of some sort, he knew how to use it. Lavender Armstrong was impressed.

She approached him at the bar, his calculator in front of his gin and tonic.

"Hi! My name is Lavender." She seated herself next to him, making sure that her thigh rubbed his in the process. He got the message.

"Can you show me how to work that? I understand it's quite complicated! You know, I have a small business, and my accountant uses one of those." He lit her Virginia Slim and commenced to run a series of numbers on the calculator. She was genuinely fascinated and kept him at the bar the rest of the evening. Even though she never asked his name, he knew that it would be the easiest piece of ass he had ever gotten.

It was.

The once empty street was now lined with cars as far as the eye could see. Carter received numerous calls from irate neighbors who complained mostly about their driveways being blocked, but he correctly guessed that they were irritated at not being invited.

Casey Scott came by limousine. It cost him fifty dollars, plus an additional two-fifty for his date. He had won in Las Vegas the previous night and was anxious to be the big spender. He contacted J. J. Hawkins, a black entrepreneur with underworld connections who ran a massage parlor on Sunset Strip. J. J. prided himself in being able to deliver whatever his clients ordered. Scott wanted a gorgeous white woman with blonde hair, and he got her! Since he seldom took his wife out, it was no surprise to the guests when he arrived without her. What was a surprise, however, was the fact that his date was so attractive. She drew mixed reactions from those present, especially the more insecure black women who didn't appreciate Scott's rent-a-white-girl idea.

Affable and outgoing, she bounced the icy stares and returned the snide comments with impunity. She was of medium height, had blue eyes and platinum-blond hair that wasn't dyed. Her skin bore the marks of a recent suntan and contrasted against the white mini-skirt she wore. She was from a wealthy family in Pennsylvania, having migrated to Los Angeles to attend the Graduate School of Social Work at UCLA. Her family's wealth had provided her with extensive travel the world over and the best education available. What it hadn't provided her with was close contact with black men, something she had longed for since her adolescent years. J. J.'s computer-dating service provided her with the vehicle she needed to exercise her fantasies. She had drawn duds on both previous dates, but Scott was the gold ring. She wasted no time in being comfortable.

Carter, drinking at the bar, couldn't help but comment to Kupp, seated on the stool next to him: "Nigger sure loves his white women, don't he?"

"For days. That's a good-looking bitch, though—huh?"

Carter shook his head, but didn't verbalize a response. Kupp finished his drink, slapped Carter on the shoulder, and started across the room to introduce himself.

Several women sitting together on the couch didn't think her presence was particularly enhancing. The one in the middle, a rather homely woman in the midst of disgust over the extramarital affair her husband was having with a white woman, was the most verbal.

"White bitch thinks she's cute—shit!" she said nudging the woman seated next to her.

"Well, you know why she's here; wants some of that black Jones!"

"Yeah, well bitch better just stay away from Mark!"

"Niggers seem to go crazy over white women, and most of them ain't nothing but trash anyway. She's kinda ugly, though. Wonder what he sees in her?"

"Yeah, and I hear he's got an ugly white woman for a wife, too. Nigger has no taste whatsoever."

"Right on!" They all laughed together and continued their gossip.

"May I get you a drink?" said Ramp as he greeted her midway across the living-room floor. She smiled, ran her comb through her hair, took him by the arm, and headed for the bar.

"My name's Chris. What's yours?"

"Carla Bennette," she responded. "I'm from Philly; go to school at UCLA."

"Hey, no kidding! My dad went to UCLA, years ago." They continued their thin dialogue at the bar as she downed a Bloody Mary.

"Hey, Carter, I want you to meet Carla. Hey, Carter—Carla; sounds funny, huh? Anyway man, she's a grad student at UCLA. Hey baby, Doc here is the host!"

"You are?" she responded. "Oh, wow! I just love your house. It really is georgeous. It's the first time that I've been in this part of the city."

Ramp couldn't resist.

"Why, blue-eyed soul sister, didn't you know that all the rich niggers live up here on the hill?"

She smiled coyly and continued drinking.

"Oh come on, Ramp, cut all that rich nigger shit out! You're embarrassing the girl."

"I'm not embarrassing her. Am I embarrassing you, Carla?" She continued to smile but said nothing.

"You see, Carter? I told you, I'm not embarrassing her!"

"Whatever you say, baby," said Carter as he continued to sip from his glass.

"Come on, Carla, let's go where we are appreciated." Ramp took her by the arm, lifted his glass to Carter for a toast, and turned to leave as Carter obliged by striking the glasses together.

Carter shook his head and smiled at the bartender, who had observed the entire exchange. It prompted him to comment, "Niggers sure do act funny around white bitches, huh?"

"Right on!"

Andrew Masters was known as the Landlord.

An older physician, he had extensive real estate holdings in Los Angeles and particularly in the Jungle, where he owned several apartment houses. He was also reputed to be the biggest pimp in the city. Behind the facade of a successful medical practice, his buildings in the Jungle earned him far in excess of what he earned as a surgeon. The one on Cocoa Street was the most lucrative because it was smaller, more lavish, and more intimate. His stable included women from all ethnic backgrounds, and all very pretty. They paid no rent, walked no streets, and spent no time in jails. He had modeled his enterprise after the ranches in Las Vegas where prostitution was legal. As a physician he kept his ladies healthy and himself wealthy. He had a built-in clientele—white physicians from the Valley, Hollywood, Beverly Hills, and the beach cities.

The apartment on Cocoa Street was surrounded by Rolls Royces, Eldorados, Mark IVs, and LTDs. He was in his mid-sixties, or so he told everyone, but he kept a youthful appearance. He had a face-lift, a hair transplant, and a new set of dentures made every year. He came to the party with a girl who was no older than twenty-five. She went by the name of Sadie Atkins. She was short, well built, wore her hair closely cropped, and had a cinnamon complexion. Masters introduced her as a friend, but everyone knew that she was the manager of the apartment on Cocoa Street. During the entire evening she flirted with every man at the party, including Carter.

Carter moved among his guests continually, talking, laughing, dancing, and joking. As the house filled to capacity, the booze flowed and the music echoed the innermost feelings of all those present. They danced to the J.B.'s, Marvin Gaye, and the Isley Brothers. They clapped their hands to the Four Tops, the Spinners, and the Temptations. Unrehearsed, they danced and finger-popped in syncopated rhythm to the music. Whatever differences existed between the grass roots and the bourgeois, this was one area where there were none. They did the soul train line, the bump, and the robot. No sooner would one record finish and they would plop down on a couch exhausted than they would be back on the floor in one mass of gyrating torsos, each in his own little world, eyes closed, heads bobbing, arms flailing, and hips rocking to the beat. They took off their shoes and coats, and slowly their masks began to crack as they let it all hang out. Regardless of parentage, affluence, or color, they all felt the same bondage; the same element of strength their forefathers had known came alive again as they identified with the music. It took them back home again, and it let them *feel,* for a time, something they each feared to do lest the mask disintegrate to an irreparable level of vulnerability.

Leviah Walker was the model physician.

From Detroit he had come to California upon discharge from the army and established himself in the late fifties. He was president of the local black medical society for a time, was a trustee of a small black college, and the author of numerous articles on hypertension in black people. He attended church regularly and was the first black man to join the Kiwanis. He lived in a modest home in Leimert Park and sent his children to Ivy League schools. He was a frequent donor to worthy causes, and, although he avoided political identification, he could be counted upon as a fundraiser for charities that demonstrated a willingness to help black people.

He took frequent vacations to the Bahamas with his family and was in a local bowling league. Dr. Walker also happened to bankroll a very successful loan-shark operation, and its revenues would guarantee that he would retire early and still maintain the life-style that he was accustomed to. Unlike Parson, he was quiet and discrete about his business ventures. But he had one weakness, and that was for young women. He met one at the party, Vashti Alexander, a social worker recently divorced from her dentist husband. She had a penchant for older men and became immediately attached to Walker. She was vivacious, engaging, and, as Walker would find out later that evening, very affectionate. In between records he approached Carter to compliment him on the party.

"This is really nice of you. Not many people open their houses up anymore. I think it's great. If I can ever be of help . . ." He would be given the chance in less than three months.

Carter was dancing with Sadie Atkins to a tune by the Staple Singers when he noticed Sable standing in the hallway, motioning for him to join her. He excused himself and danced slowly in step with the music over to where she was standing.

"Hey baby, looking mighty good tonight!" He kissed her behind the ear and tried to rub her buttocks, which she stopped by grabbing his wrist. Carter left her and joined a group at the bar that was hysterical with laughter after hearing an episode related by Angel. He insisted on having it repeated and got all of the cooperation he needed.

"You remember that shoot-out in a Harlem bar few years back? Between the cops and the niggers—across the street from Harlem Hospital? Well, cops blew about four niggers away, and there were bodies all over the floor, see, and so when the smoke cleared . . ." Angel had to stop because, like his audience, he couldn't control his laughter. "And so when the smoke cleared and the cops came into the bar, the rest of the niggers in the bar were stepping over the dead bodies. . . ."

Carter interrupted. "What's so unusual about stepping over dead bodies?" The group screamed with laughter.

"But that's what's so funny, Carter," Angel continued, wiping the tears from his eyes. "Niggers were stepping over the bodies on their way to the bar to get another *drink!* Now you know that's a goddamn shame; niggers ain't got no respect for the dead brothers. Stepped over the motherfuckers on the way"—his voice cut off by the deafening sound of the audience as they joined him in hysterics— "stepped over the niggers on the way to the bar. Niggers ain't shit!" Carter found himself laughing along with them, although he wasn't sure if he was amused by the story or by the people listening to it.

By now everyone was feeling pretty mellow, most from the booze and a few from grass. It was after one, and the tempo of the party was changing. They wanted to hear more Roberta Flack and Isaac Hayes, more Grover Washington, Jr., and Donald Byrd. Carter circulated through his entourage, returned the flirtations of Sadie Atkins, listened to the lies that Angel told, started a game of chess with Bannister, pulled Scott's date out of the pool, and spent the rest of the evening changing LP's and looking at the cleavage on Angel's date.

Al Green had just finished the first cut on his new album when the interlude was broken by a piercing scream accompanied by the sound of broken glass and falling silverware coming from the direction of the kitchen. Carter reached the kitchen a step ahead of Leviah Walker, whom he had been talking to only moments before.

Janice lay writhing on the tile, her eyes protruding and blood oozing down the corners of her mouth. The floor was strewn with hors d'oeurvres and napkins while the splintered remains of the punch bowl lay scattered about the counter top, its contents dripping slowly into a puddle on the floor next to her head.

The young intern was bending over Janice trying to force the handle of a serving spoon between her teeth, but the jerking movements of her limbs made it difficult.

Walker secured her head while Carter restrained her arms, the intern still struggling to get the spoon handle between her teeth.

"What the hell you running here, Carter, a goddamn general hospital?" asked Bannister, peering through the door, now packed with guests.

"No shit! Seems like it, huh!"

Walker grabbed a napkin and wiped the foam from around her

mouth, its mixture with the blood giving it an opalescent appearance. She began emitting a hissinglike sound as the intern finally pried open her mouth and inserted the spoon handle. The bluish color in her face began to disappear as she breathed more easily.

The intern wiped the sweat from his forehead as he spoke. "Damn, she was really cyanotic. Wow! We were just talking, she was getting ready to take the tray into the room and all of a sudden— pow! Scared the *shit* out of me until I realized what happened."

"Sable, get my bag out of the bedroom, stat, baby!" Carter said.

"You got any Nembutal, man?" Walker asked, still holding her head.

"No, but I have some Valium. Ten milligrams IV should do it till she gets to the hospital."

"Sounds all right. She's a big chick. You'll have a hell of a time finding a vein, though."

"I'm hip!"

Sable returned with the bag, and Carter fished for the syringe and the vial. He tore open a small packet that contained an alcohol-impregnated gauze and commenced to wipe the skin of the arm that he was restraining. Sable requested everyone to return to the party in order to clear the kitchen. Carter made several blind stabs with the needle before successfully getting a vein. Janice's extremities jerked in rhythmic contractions, and her fingers were in boardlike rigidity.

"Sable! Janice ever say she had epilepsy?" Carter asked, compressing the area of the injection to keep it from hemorrhaging.

"No, baby, she never mentioned anything to me. In fact, she bragged about how good her health was despite her obesity. She never told me anything. Course, I wasn't that close to her. I mean, we're good friends and all that, but . . ."

"Go look in her purse; see if there's any medicine bottles or whatever."

"Would you suspect a brain tumor if her history is negative for previous seizures?" the young intern asked.

"I'm sorry, I don't remember your name," Carter said, slightly embarrassed. "You're an intern at King, aren't you?"

"Yes. Nelson, David Nelson."

"Well, Dr. Nelson, I think that's one of the things you have to rule out, along with drug withdrawal, particularly the barbs. She might have a fistula, aneurysm—it's hard to say. But yes, a space-occupying lesion has to be considered in the absence of any history of convulsions."

"Well, you can rule out withdrawal!" Sable snapped, having returned to the kitchen. "She's not a junkie, I'm sure of that!"

"Nobody said she was, baby! You just have to rule out a drug history, that's all! Look, get admitting on the phone at the hospital so we can get her over there. You find anything in her purse?"

"Nope."

The convulsion let up shortly after the injection of Valium. As her limbs became flaccid, she began to breathe deeply,the harsh, resonating sound from her throat echoing through the kitchen.

"She's postical now: won't come out of it till she gets to the hospital," Walker said. "If you gentlemen don't need me, I need a drink and so will excuse myself to achieve that goal."

"Be my guest, Dr. Walker, by all means." Carter and Walker stood up and bowed to each other like eighteenth-century knights.

"Strange," said Sable. "Very strange!"

The crisis over, Carter returned to his guests while Dr. Nelson remained in the kitchen with Janice until the ambulance arrived a short time later. Sable and Vashti reconstructed the kitchen and joined the crowd.

After the ambulance left for the hospital with Ramp and Janice, Carter made a pronouncement: "All niggers must have a physical examination before you come into this house." Lavender took it from there. Shouting from the bar, she broke the crowd up with laughter. "Did you say we have to *come* in your house or come *into* your house?"

That was all that Calvin needed. "No, baby, he said all niggers have to come—*period!*"

"I didn't hear him say that," said Angel. "I'm sure he said that niggers are supposed to come in their *own* houses." The crowd was hysterical now, the final release before they had to put the masks back on and return to their push-button domiciles and credit-card neuroses.

They continued their vulgarities until they were exhausted and at two-thirty began leaving as they had arrived, the ark emptying into the promised land. A few lingered for a last drink or a last effort to line up a good screw to top off the evening. Calvin and Scott stood outside in the driveway, shouting at the top of their lungs about who would win the Freedom Classic on Sunday.

As the last guest left, Carter and Sable surveyed the damage; a broken punch bowl, a cigarette burn in the rug by the window, and several spilled drinks on the wall near the stereo—all repairable.

It took the two of them twenty minutes to clean up the living room and den.

They were dressing for bed when the phone rang. Thinking that it was Ramp calling from the hospital, Sable answered. It was Carter's exchange, and there was a call from Damon Wilson, an emergency! She gave him the receiver. He listened while Damon spoke rapidly, frequently stuttering as he spoke. He had information that he was sure was related to Jimmie's murder and wanted to discuss it tonight. No! It could not wait until next week! Carter tried unsuccessfully to put him off until Sunday afternoon, finally agreeing to a meeting if Damon could get transportation there. Carter was too high to drive anywhere. Damon hung up the receiver without saying good-bye. Sable, having overheard the conversation, questioned him about the murder.

"I'd almost forgotten about it. Son of a woman that works at the Center had a friend get killed. Kinda strange at that—and, know what? During the funeral I think we were followed, but . . ." He hesitated, yawning as he slipped his robe on. "Maybe it was just my imagination." He shrugged his shoulders and sat on the edge of the bed.

"If I were you I'd listen to the man, baby. Shit! They might be after you!" It was the first time the thought crossed his mind, and it made him uncomfortable. Sable sensed his uneasiness and tried to neutralize it. She reached across the bed and began massaging his neck, her thin fingers working the heavy muscles like a trainer preparing his fighter for the main event.

"How 'bout some coffee? Keep you awake till he gets here."

"I can dig it." She moved her arms around his chest and squeezed, kissing him on the neck before she left the room. The aroma of coffee soon filled the air, accompanied by the sounds of the Jazz Crusaders as they diffused harmoniously together throughout the house.

Carter cursed himself for having agreed to meet Damon this time of morning. After all, it could have waited. He thought about his guests who by now were sound asleep in their hillside cavities dreaming of tomorrow. He planned to do the same, just as soon as Damon said his piece.

He guessed it wouldn't take more than an hour.

CHAPTER 7

THE BELL RANG at 5:00 A.M. and two figures, casting ghost-like shadows against the door, stood shivering before the porch light. The Yellow Cab sat idling in the street behind them, its parking lights blinking like a neon sign.

"Gimme six dollars for the cab," Damon said, his outstretched palm in front of him. Carter went through his pockets and then went to the den where he kept his wallet, returning with six one-dollar bills. He watched Damon put one in his pocket and give the other five to the driver.

"How did you get a cab this time of night, or should I say morning?" He glanced at his watch as he closed the door and escorted them to the living room.

"Shit! Wasn't easy! We had to walk over to Century near the freeway, and just happened it was a brother. He was bent out of shape until I gave him your address. Then he . . . oh hey, look, sorry, this is my partner, Leon. I would've been here sooner, but this nigger didn't want to come!"

Carter extended his hand to Leon, who grabbed it indifferently if not contemptuously.

Sable emerged from the kitchen with a silver tray that contained a pot of coffee and four cups. "Would you men like some coffee?"

"This is my lady, Sable. Sable this is Damon and . . ." He hesitated, waiting for Leon to prompt him but remembered the name before he could speak. "Leon, yeah," he said, snapped his fingers and seated himself in the recliner next to Sable. "You have any objections if she listens?"

"Don't make me no never mind," said Damon, looking at Leon for approval. Leon shrugged his shoulders, indicating agreement, and continued to drink his coffee. His eyes scanned the house like a camera on a tripod. He had nothing but contempt for bourgeois blacks, especially doctors, and although it was apparent to Carter, he would not find out why for some time.

They sat silently facing one another, each waiting for the other to speak, sipping their coffee, trying to pretend they were at ease.

Sable took the initiative.

"It's pretty late. Folks know where you are?" Damon nodded his head and continued to drink from the cup that steamed in front of him.

"Like I was saying, I would've been here sooner, but the nigger here didn't want to come. I almost had to jack him up—shit! Some niggers are just plain *dumb!*"

"What the hell you want to jam *me* for, nigger?" Leon snapped, his indifferent face becoming surly. He continued to sip his coffee in silence.

"Now gentlemen, it's very late, and I know you didn't come all the way up here just to drink coffee, so without further bullshitting, can we get on with it, please?" Carter was tired and irritated, his patience wearing thin. "You said something about having some info about Jimmie or whatever."

Damon became anxious, moving and twisting on the couch, pulling his socks up and winding his watch.

"I'm waiting! Don't everyone speak at once!" Carter said sarcastically. Sable jabbed an elbow in his side, indicating her displeasure at his attitude. He looked at her a moment and then took a softer line.

"Hey, look here, if you guys want to rap about it tomorrow you can sack out here for tonight, have breakfast in the morning. Hell, it'll be daylight in an hour or so."

The boys looked at each other for a second or so, their eyes shifting to the table in front of them.

"Well . . ." Damon, trying to rub the fatigue out of his eyes with the palm of his hand, continued: "You get a copy of last week's—no, two week's ago's, *Sentinel*? The one that came out just 'fore Jimmie got killed?"

Carter looked at Sable and shook his head, responding, "No, I don't believe so."

"Wait a minute, honey," said Sable, moving off the arm of the recliner. "You got a whole pile of old papers on the back porch, including the *Sentinel*. I don't know what date, though. You know what date, Leon?" Leon didn't know, but it was important that he appear as if he knew, so he looked at Damon as if trying to remind himself.

Carter saw right through it and suggested that Sable bring all the papers into the room. She spread them out on the rug next to the coffee table and began to put them in order by dates.

"Look for the one that has the school in the headlines," said Damon.

"What about the school?" said Carter.

"Just look at the headlines."

"Is this it?" said Sable as she threw a folded newspaper on the table, the headlines reading "VANDALS DO $50,000 DAMAGE TO 103RD STREET SCHOOL."

"Yeah, yeah, that's the one," said Damon, handing the paper to Carter.

He read the article under the headline relating the incident of classroom damage. It wasn't a long article; it had relatively few facts and a mere conjecture as to motive.

"So what about it?" Carter continued to press.

Damon looked at Leon once again before speaking, and when he did, he was clear, though hesitant.

"Well, it . . . was us, Doc. I mean we're—well, Buddy, Leon, Jimmie, Arthur, and me—was the ones who did the school thing. You understand what I'm saying?"

Carter looked at them with a glum expression. He tried to see their eyes, but they avoided him, looking to either side in shame. He tried not to be judgmental, so quickly moved the dialogue ahead.

"So! What's that got to do with Jimmie's murder?"

Damon turned to Leon, jabbing him with his elbow. "So tell him, tell him what he said!"

Leon looked up for a moment, his eyes trapped by Carter's stare, then looked back at Damon for support.

"Tell him what he *said!*"

"You ain't gonna call the cops are you?" said Leon, sitting up for the first time on the couch.

"No!"

"Tell him about the *call!*"

"Well, Jimmie called me the night before, you know, before we was suppose' to meet, and said that he had found something in the basement of the school that week before but didn't know if he should tell anyone. He said that he was scared of what they might do to him, and he wanted to tell us about it. I thought he was talking about having to go to camp or something like that. I didn't realize he was talking about getting *killed*—shit! He said he'd tell us about it in the morning. That's when we found him wiped out!"

Carter was now wide awake.

"Did he say anything else, anything at all that might give you a clue as to what it was? I mean, did he say it was something he took or something that's still there?"

"He didn't say *nothin'* else. Just that he'd tell us about it in the morning. I didn't think nothin' of it. Hell, I thought he might have found one of the teachers screwing or something!"

"Well who else was with him?" Sable asked.

"That's just it, miss, wasn't no one with him. We was all up in the classrooms. He was the only one that went in the basement. Didn't none of us go with him. He was coming up the stairs as we was leaving 'cause we thought we heard someone coming, so we all split quick! Didn't none of us hear from him till the next week. He didn't tell no one but Leon about the basement thing," volunteered Damon.

"Did he seem scared when he called you, Leon?" Carter asked, searching for more information.

"Like I said, he just talked about being scared of what they might *do* to him. He seemed kinda casual about it, though, said it could wait."

"Who is 'they'?"

"What?"

"You said he was afraid of what 'they' might do. Who is 'they'?"

"Oh, I dunno! Whoever he saw in the basement, I guess. Shit! Don't ask *me!*"

"Are you sure he didn't say anything else that might give you a clue to what he was talking about?"

Leon shook his head and continued to drink his coffee, the steam fogging his glasses as he held the cup just below his chin. Carter sat pensively for a moment, his eyes fixed on the youngsters seated in front of him. He was uncertain as to what to do. They had come to him because they trusted him; at least, he was sure Damon did. Leon was reluctant to talk, and he wanted to know why. So he pushed and found out in short order.

"How come you didn't want to rap with us tonight, Leon?" he asked.

Leon's answer was quick and to the point. "Shit, *I* don't want to get killed. What the fuck you *think?*"

"But you don't know that the school thing *is* the reason he got killed."

"Shit! Look, Doc, you keep believing that. OK? Wasn't no *other* reason for him to get wasted. Nigger had four dollars in his pocket that wasn't touched. An' 'sides, he *said* it was anyway."

"Don't you see, Doc," Damon said, his eyes widening as he sought to convince Carter, "it has to be the school, it just has to be!"

Sable needed no convincing. Her previous experiences left her with the realization that one best trust his own intuition and not necessarily logic.

"If what they say is true, it makes sense, honey."

"You tell Leon about the funeral?" Carter said, directing his comment to Damon.

Like Carter, Damon had forgotten about the incident. Leon listened intently as the sequence of events was related. Damon was

87

a bit dramatic in his presentation, but none the less accurate. It was at that point that Leon's fear came out into the open.

"That means if they followed *you*, they must know about me an' Arthur—shit! Any one of us might be next. Damn! That means we just sittin' ducks, man!"

It was the first time that Carter realized the value in Leon's apprehension. If they were trying to finger everyone Jimmie had talked to, then they might very well finger him because of his association with Damon. He felt the goose bumps break out over his body as they talked, but he kept his own fear inside. The connection between the ghetto school and Jimmie's death was remote, but if it was true, then Leon might well have a point. The youngsters were becoming more panicky the more they talked, so Carter tried to relieve their feelings. He had little luck, primarily because his own concern was beginning to show.

They talked until morning came as an uninvited guest, its rays of sun falling on the rug in latticelike formation as Sable opened the drapes in the den. They were all tired but too keyed up to sleep. She had no trouble convincing everyone to have breakfast.

Leon ate voraciously, asking for seconds only after he felt he could do so without embarrassment. Although the meal was good, Carter ate in strange silence, his thoughts turning over in his mind all that had transpired. He was hesitant to ask his next question but felt it was necessary: "You gonna mention this to your folks?"

"Hell, no!" said Damon emphatically.

"For all you know, the cops might be in on it, whatever it is," said Sable, regarding Carter sharply out of the corners of her eyes.

"Right on, sister Sable," said Leon, raising a clenched fist. For some strange reason he liked her. Perhaps it was because she seemed to understand what he was saying. He didn't have to explain things to her the way he did to Carter. Although he disliked bourgeois blacks, she came on differently—she was more sincere, he guessed. He wasn't so sure about her old man, although he was becoming more comfortable around him. Having finished breakfast, he decided to test Carter to see how real he was. He got more than he bargained for.

"Say, Doc, tell me something. How much a pad like this cost, huh?"

"Enough. Why do you ask?"

"Curious to know how many niggers you had to rip off to get something like this, that's all."

"Why do I have to rip off anyone to get a house?"

"Well, the man ain't giving nothing away, so the only way you could get something like this is rip off the brothers—shit!"

"You got a problem."

"How so? I mean, all you middle-class niggers come down to the ghetto in your Mark IV's and hogs, trying to look good and don't do nothing for black folks but rip them off!"

Leon's last comment irritated Carter, although it was what he expected.

"Look, man, do you know what happens when black doctors go to the ghetto? Let me give you an example so you can see how misguided you are! Last week a kid eighteen was in an auto wreck, OK? Mother brought him in the ambulance to the Center. Kid's trachea, his windpipe, was broken, and he couldn't breathe—right! Lots of bleeding from the injured tissue went into the windpipe, understand? OK, so I cut a hole below where it was broken and put a metal tube in so he could breathe, 'cause he was damn near dead by the time I got to him in the first place. I stayed with that dude damn near all night, assisted the surgeon with the repair, transfused him six pints of blood, and . . ."

Leon interrupted him. "But you're a doctor! That's what you suppose' to do!"

"Right on! But let me finish the story, OK?"

Leon conceded, and Carter lit a cigarette before continuing.

"So I stayed with this kid most of the night till he went into the recovery room after the operation. When I went out into the waiting room to tell his mother that he was going to be all right, you know what she said?

"'Well I'm glad you saved his life, but I want him taken to Kaiser where the *white* people can look out for him.' Can you imagine that shit! Stay up all night to save the dude's life just to hear *that!*" The room was tense as Carter talked, his anger just below the boiling point.

"Well, Doc, that was an exception."

"Exception, my ass. That's the way it is in general in any black community. Black professionals who work in the ghetto know that ahead of time. Isn't a day that I go to work that I don't expect to get cussed out or something, but I understand now. I didn't at first. I don't look for gratitude although I get it at times, but black folks suffer, man—we suffer like motherfuckers! My gratitude comes from the results of my work even if the patients don't recognize it. But the tragedy, the real tragedy is the brainwashing that whitey has done on us, including you, baby!" Carter pointed his finger at Leon, which made him anxious.

"Shit, I ain't brainwashed. Don't know what you talking about!"

"Bullshit if you aren't. You wouldn't have asked me that question if you didn't believe it in the first place, man!"

Leon tried to modify his position but put his foot in the middle of the shit. "But you're different. The rest of them dudes ain't that way."

"Oh come on, Leon, get off that 'different' shit! That's jive stuff that whitey put on us, man! Can't you see the game? He's got you convinced that middle-class niggers are different, and what's worse, he got middle-class niggers believing that they different, too—shit! You think that just because a cat is bourgeois that he's free?" Leon sat in silence, overwhelmed, but before he could gather his thoughts, Carter grabbed his arm and pulled him toward the door that led to the garage.

"Look at that!" he said angrily, pulling off the cover to the Ferrari. "Look at that! That's a twenty-thousand-dollar car. Does that make me free?"

Leon stared momentarily and started to speak: "Well, I meant . . ."

But Carter grabbed his shirtsleeve before he could finish and pulled him toward the back of the house and out on the patio next to the pool. "That's a pool by Paddock. Does it make me free? No, motherfucker, it does not! My skin is the same color as yours, and we both in the same boat together. If you drown, so do I; if I drown, so do you. Dig it? You got to stop believing all that shit the man puts out. They'll call me a nigger just as fast as they call you one—OK?"

Leon shrugged his shoulders as if to say, What next? Having found all avenues for comment cut off, he managed a weak smile as he looked at Carter, surprised at first, then puzzled. He still thought Carter was different.

Carter placed a hand on his shoulder as they walked back toward the house. He had been a little heavy on Leon, although he deserved it, but he didn't want to antagonize him. He spoke in a much more subdued tone.

"Didn't mean to blow up at you, man, but I guess it's just that I care so much about black folks that I hate to see us at each other's throats."

Leon's thoughts didn't change a bit. There was still something different about him. He felt that a lot of what Carter had said was bullshit, but for now he would let it stand.

Sable had finished the dishes and returned to the den, where Damon was snoring on the rug. Leon tapped him on the arm, and he awakened, startled, as he tried to regain his orientation.

"You cats get through arguing?" he said as he yawned.

"We weren't arguing, man—just talking about the brothers, that's all."

"Whatever you say, my man." The stereo was bellowing spirituals, so Sable switched to albums and put on one by Al Green. It was soothing, just like the quiet before the storm.

"So what do you think we ought to do about the school, Doc?" Damon asked.

"I think we should tell someone, or better yet, get some advice from somebody who can be objective."

"You ain't gonna tell the pigs. . . ?"

"No, Leon, I ain't gonna tell the pigs! But I do have a friend in mind that has some sense. Want to meet him?"

"He a brother?"

"Of course he is. What the hell you think!"

"Yeah, well, you know . . ."

"Who are you talking about? Mathis?" Sable asked.

"Yeah. How'd you know, baby?"

"Who the hell else you gonna tell, Mary Poppins?"

"Very funny." Sable rubbed his neck as they laughed, her soft hands like a jacuzzi as they massaged his aching muscles.

"He's a guy I know who used to be in the service, in demolition or something like that. He's a cool dude. You can trust him."

Carter knew that they were already questioning their wisdom in telling him about the school. He thought he had convinced them of his sincerity, but it was obvious they still were uneasy with him, especially Leon.

Leon trusted no one, and it was significant that he was there with them. A child of the ghetto, he had little contact with the outside world except by radio and TV. He had no one at home to motivate him toward anything except the elements of survival, a skill that he, like other black folks, had developed to an exceptionally high level of sophistication. He had a small circle of peers, some of whom came and went, but he knew them each well; he knew where they were coming from, and, more importantly, he knew where he stood with them.

But Carter had been right.

Leon had no exposure to black bourgeois except what he heard passed from mouth to mouth. It wasn't good. That's why Carter's attitude surprised him; it wasn't quite like he had heard. But he would lay back and be his cool self and see before passing judgment.

It turned out to be a lazy day. Mathis wouldn't be available until that evening, so Leon and Damon spent the day in the pool. Carter purchased swim trunks for them that morning and gave each one a ride in the Ferrari. Sable fixed lunch for them and returned to bed for the rest of the afternoon. It was the first time that either of them had been in a private pool, their previous activity having always been confined to what few public pools there were in the ghetto. Although not admitting it, they were ecstatic, their raucous laughter exploding in stacattolike fashion, interrupted only by the sounds of splashing water and the overmodulated transistor radio perched on the diving board. It was a smog-free day, and the hot sun burned into their flesh as they lay sprawled on the deck beside the pool. They pushed, splashed, raced, and dunked each other continually and for the first time felt free of the harassment by a life guard's whistle and the intimidation of gangs. It was dusk when Carter finally reached Mathis by phone. He had some things to do first, but he agreed to drop by when he was finished.

In the interim they ate dinner.

Sable had slept late, and so Carter spared her the anguish of cooking by bringing home food from the nearby Golden Bird. The activities of the day had taken their minds off of the events at hand, but when Mathis arrived they returned to the reality of their thoughts and fears.

Mathis's appearance was quite out of character for the work he was in. His blue Chevelle was in a bad state of disrepair, the muffler bellowing smoke like an incinerator. He was a tall, swarthy man with coarse features. He wore his hair closely cut out of habit, the military having given him no options. His speech was even less impressive than his appearance, but that was deceptive, because he used it to his advantage in dealing with street people. As a drug rehabilitation counselor, he was none the less effective because it was easy to identify with him. He was nonpretentious and unassuming in his manner. His dress was conservative, perhaps the strangest thing about him. His suits were out of style and ill-fitting. His shoes archaic. He was athletically inclined and spent his spare time jogging and weight lifting. It kept him in excellent physical condition, something that would be to his advantage in the next few months. He was still in his sweatsuit when he arrived at Carter's, the musty odor a sharp contrast to the fragrance of incense that constantly burned in the den, something that Sable picked up during her college years.

He greeted Sable affectionately, kissing her on the cheek as he entered the house. She led him to the den where the others were seated, and after brief introductions they began discussing the series of events that had taken place before his involvement.

Mathis listened intently as Damon once again repeated all that had happened, this time a little less dramatically. He had no questions, comments, or opinions while Damon spoke. The more he heard, the more intrigued he became. Nine years in the army as an intelligence officer taught him several things, two of which remained etched in his mind: never jump to conclusions, and never believe all of what you hear until you see for yourself and then question it afterward. His first remark shocked everyone, including Carter.

"I think someone else is going to get killed before it's over," he said, his face expressionless. The remark sent a chill through Carter, who up to this point hadn't given the incident much credence.

"Why do you say that? I mean, we don't know if there's anything in the school that's connected to the kid's murder?"

"I agree, so there's only one way to find out for sure, isn't there!"

"What? Tell the cops?" asked Leon, panicky. Mathis shook his head slowly, carefully planning his next statement, which he knew would throw them.

"Nope! Got something else in mind, I think . . ."

"Tell the principal," Damon volunteered spontaneously, as if he were playing twenty questions.

Mathis continued undaunted: "I think someone has to go back down into that basement and see what's there. Whatever it is, if anything, got someone killed and may get someone else killed."

"Like who, for instance?" Leon asked, his hands trembling as he sat on the edge of his chair. Mathis shrugged his shoulders but did not answer.

"What do you mean, 'Someone has to go into the basement'? Why can't the principal do it?" Carter's anxiety was beginning to show. Mathis's next answer only made it worse.

"Suppose you do that—tell the principal, I mean—and he calls the police, which he'll do of course, but suppose he finds a cache of heroin in the basement? How are you going to explain—better yet, how would you convince them that you had no advance knowledge, especially when you're the one that told them about it?"

"Aw, there ain't no heroin down there," Carter said, himself shaken.

"Who are you trying to convince, baby, me or you? No, gentlemen, I'm afraid that you're the ones that will have to do it." Mathis was no longer relaxed in his chair now, but stiff, poised, and focused.

They would not have to ask him to help them. He would jump at the chance. It was almost like the army days where there had always been the mystery, the challenge of the unknown. The more he thought about it, the more he listened, the more exciting it sounded. He had done such things thousands of times before—breaking into offices to get evidence, setting people up, planting information on them that would insure a legitimate outcome in behalf of the government. His sadistic personality thrived on the anticipation of the kill, the capture of the quarry. It made no difference that the tactics were unethical—or illegal, for that matter. But that ended when he was discharged from the service. It was something he had never gotten over, something that left a bitter taste in his mouth. He had served his country loyally, and his only reward was a dishonorable discharge after nine years. Nine years out of his life that he could have spent in school or in some other effort. But the word of a senior officer, bigoted as they came, was all that was needed to maximize a minor infraction and turn it into a dishonorable discharge. He would never forget that and vowed never to enter that line of work again, but the discussion before him rekindled feelings that longed to be fanned.

"You mean we have to break into the school again?" Damon asked in disbelief.

"That's what I said."

"You're crazy! You're out of your mind! We got away with it once 'cause it was just a prank. I mean, we was lucky 'cause we didn't know what we was doing, but to do it again on purpose . . . ?"

Mathis interrupted. "So don't do it!" he said matter-of-factly.

"But you said someone might end up getting killed!"

"Might end up getting killed if you go down there, but at least you stand a better chance by knowing what it's all about. Take your choice. I'll be glad to help, but I suggest that it be soon."

"You'll never get me into that school. No, Lord! I may be dumb. But, baby, I ain't no *fool!* I'll have to take my chances on the street, but I'll be goddamned if I'm going back in *there!*" Leon jumped up from his seat, his hand still trembling. He paced as he talked, his anxiety overwhelming.

"The rest of you feel that way?" Mathis asked, sizing up his force. Damon remained silent, his fear having paralyzed his thoughts. Carter was uncertain, still not convinced that there was much to be worried about.

"I'll go with you!" Sable's voice was strong and committed. A startled Carter looked at her in disbelief.

"Baby, you know what you're *saying?* I mean, goddamn, honey, I don't want you involved!"

"Shit, I'm already involved. This is right up my alley."

"You saying that just 'cause I'm not sure?"

"No! You have to make your own decision, baby."

"Yeah, well look here, Mathis, count me in. I sure as hell ain't gonna let anything happen to her. I'll go, shit yeah, I'll go. And *you* will keep your black ass out of there!" Carter said, pointing his finger at Sable. She smiled innocently and winked.

"I could stand guard," she said.

"Really will!"

"He's got a point, Sable. We're going into it blind. No telling what's down there, if anything." He paused a moment. There was a look of reservation in his eyes. He looked about the den. Its rosewood-paneled walls, covered with black art, mirrored the dancing images cast by the reflected light from the adjacent pool. "You know," he began, his unlit cigarette dangling from his lips like a pacifier, "this will take a little planning. And the more I think about it, the more I think only a few should go, preferably only two— well, really only one, but I guess two would be OK."

"Do we really have to do this?" Damon asked, perplexed.

Mathis lit his cigarette and assumed a comfortable position in the chair, all the while his head tilting back as he eyed Damon over the bridge of his nose. He exhaled a puff of smoke arrogantly from his pursed lips and watched it rise slowly. "Like I said, my man, you don't have to do anything. I'm not in favor of kids getting involved at this point, but I would like for you to tell me as much as you can about the school."

"How you mean?" Damon said, looking at Leon indifferently.

"Well, for one, how you got in. Why don't you draw me a map or a diagram of the place? I need to know how the corridors are laid out and where the entrances and staircases are located."

"Oh, that's easy. The door to the rear of the main classroom building on the ground floor is all-steel, but the molding is separated from the . . ." Mathis cut him off, his voice impatient.

"Draw me a diagram!"

"I will, I will, but let me explain how you have to get in first," he demanded. "The door is separated from the molding so far that all you have to do is take a metal bar or something and force it open. It's easy!"

As Damon talked, Mathis fished through magazines that lay on the table before him, then gestured for Sable to bring him something to write on. She responded quickly with several sheets of lined paper and a felt-tipped pen. Mathis, without speaking, reached across the table, his steady hand holding the paper provocatively in front of Damon.

"Draw me a *diagram!*" he repeated when Damon finished speaking.

"I ain't no artist, man!" he said, smiling sheepishly.

"This isn't an art contest. Just draw me a diagram!" said Mathis insistently.

To everyone's surprise, Damon's schematic was well done. It was three-dimensional as well as shaded. It prompted Sable to ask if he had ever taken art or drafting in school. He replied in the negative. His talent had obviously gone unrecognized by the indifferent school system, its purpose more concerned with discipline than with nurturing creative talent.

He explained the details of the diagram thoroughly. Since neither he nor Leon had gone to the basement, that part of the diagram was blank. Only the stairwell leading to the basement was included. Mathis had him draw the layout for each floor and each section of the school, including buildings far removed from the central classrooms.

It was an unusual design for a school, particularly for a ghetto school. Its open-air cafeteria and cantilevered roof structure were of recent vintage. It was the only new structure in Watts south of the railroad tracks, with the exception of its neighbor, Mafundi, whose own design was equally appealing. Together they stood as symbols. In their infancy they were born out of frustration and necessity, which came with the awareness of black pride and of a system bent on oppressing it.

Carefully and meticulously Mathis planned the break-in. In light of the fact that the school had been vandalized previously, they should anticipate a stricter security system. He planned to enter the yard from the 103rd Street side.

That bothered Carter.

"But that's a busy street! We're bound to be seen by someone. Why you want to go in that way?"

"Simple. The central classrooms are on the corner of 103rd and Grape streets, OK? The basement is directly below the central classrooms. Now if we enter from Wilmington or Beach streets, we have to cross the entire distance of the playground. A chain-link fence doesn't offer much protection, does it?"

Carter sighed, looked for a brief moment toward the pool, and then at the faces in the room. He cleared his throat before speaking. "I'm still not clear on why you want to go in from a busy street."

"Let me finish," Mathis said, lighting another cigarette. "If we try and enter from the Grape Street side, we're staring into the bedrooms of the projects, right? Now, no matter what time we enter, there's always going to be niggers up at that hour. Our chances of getting caught would be too great!"

"Well, *we* entered from that side and didn't get caught!" said Leon, his eyes sweeping the room for support.

"That's right, you did. But it was daylight, and you were playing basketball until it got dark. I must admit, it was a natural cover. Besides, it wasn't planned, was it? It just happened, right?"

"Well . . . yeah . . . I guess so," Leon said in a reflecting voice.

"OK. So let's move on. If we enter from the 103rd Street side, we minimize any chance of being seen because facing the school ain't nothing but small shops and shit. Right? Ain't nothing but shoe stores, a grocery, and some jive-ass real estate offices. Hey, they'll all be closed by the time we get ready to move. I mean, goddamn, if a motherfucker is fixing shoes at three in the morning, then we all deserve to get caught—shit!" Laughter exploded in the den as Mathis smiled while blowing smoke toward the ceiling.

When the noise subsided, he continued: "We'll arrange to be at Mafundi during the night until we're ready to move. That'll minimize travel, give us plenty of time to rest, and observe the school unnoticed. It'll also give us a chance to plan for any contingencies should they arise."

"What's that?" Damon asked, puzzled.

"Just means a change in plans in case it's necessary."

"Will Mafundi cooperate?" asked Sable.

"Don't see why not," Mathis said, clasping his hands behind his head. "I'll arrange all that, though. Shouldn't be a problem."

"How long we gonna be in there?" Carter asked. Mathis looked at Damon and inquired how long they had been in the classrooms that night. He guessed it had been no more than thirty minutes.

"That should be long enough for us. Sable, you'll be in the car parked directly in front of the school. I'll arrange walkie-talkies for us, just in case something comes up."

"What do I do if you get into trouble down there?" she asked, a slight bit of apprehension noticeable in her voice.

He hadn't completely worked it out, but he sought to calm her anxieties. "I'll probably arrange to have someone at Mafundi you can notify, but—" he hesitated, and then laughed as he finished his sentence—"the likelihood of anything like that happening is so remote that I don't see any reason to worry about it. Stop making something out of nothing, OK?"

"Well, but you don't know that, man. I mean, we should have some kind of protection. After all, the way you're planning this thing makes it sound like a James Bond adventure—shit!" said Carter, his voice uneasy and searching for reassurance.

Mathis sensed it and responded: "If you want me to tell you that it's absolutely risk free, I can't. Hell, man, I don't know if there's any connection between the school and that *kid's* death, but have you got a better idea?"

"No!"

Mathis shrugged his shoulders and looked about the den indifferently.

"When do you want to do it?" Sable asked.

"The festival is about ten days away. Too much traffic on 103rd, and the park will be crowded. First Wednesday night after it's over, and preferably a night that it rains."

"Suppose it don't rain?" Leon asked cynically.

"Then we wait! Simple as that."

"Why do you want it to rain?" Sable asked.

Mathis looked at her across the table, his eyes fixed on hers. As he opened his mouth to speak, she waved him silent with her hand, exclaiming: "Never mind! I know, I just wasn't thinking—sorry! Niggers *definitely* stay inside when it rains." She smiled sheepishly and returned to her drink.

"We need to bring anything with us?" Carter asked, swirling the glass of bourbon before his eyes.

"Just yourself, my man."

They continued to talk loosely for about an hour and then broke up. Mathis agreed to take the boys home. They were to say nothing to anyone about the conversation. He would call Carter when the time was right, and they would go from there. It had been a long day and everyone was tired, but each lingered with an air of uneasy anticipation. Something was going to happen, and they would be involved. But how? What was in the school, or was it just a misinterpretation of a youngster's fantasy?

Carter was silent as he watched the taillights disappear down the street. Sable joined him in the doorway, her arms around his waist. She rested her head between his shoulder blades and slowly rubbed her breasts across his back repeatedly.

"You know something," she said softly, "I think this whole thing is absurd. I mean, about all anyone is going to find in a school basement is some boilers and an alley cat with a litter of kittens."

Carter turned slowly in her arms, gently caressing her back as he closed the door and walked slowly toward the bedroom.

"I'm inclined to agree with you," he said as he kissed her on the neck, her robe falling gracefully to the floor. "Nothing but an alley cat and a litter of kittens!"

CHAPTER 8

THE FESTIVAL CAME with its carpetbaggers, politicians, and police. It was a combination that seldom changed down through the years, but the underpinnings of the festival had slowly been eroded and, like termites, the remaining structure was nothing but a shell of broken dreams, empty words, and hollow promises. But it was a place to go and became the center of activity in the hot August sun. Will Rogers Park on the corner of 103rd Street and Central Avenue had been renamed Malcolm X Park, and although the city fathers had not approved, the residents of Watts could care less. They had long since stopped asking government officials for permission to change their destiny. A crudely lettered sign was tacked to the stump of a tree: MALCOLM X PARK FOR THE PEOPLE!

Wooden platforms lined the perimeter of the park, and brightly colored tents filled the interior. The gymnasium housed the artwork, always a high point of the festival and one of the few remnants still carrying with it the meaning of what the festival was originally about.

The festival was like a magnet drawing patronizing housewives of bigoted Beverly Hills executives who sought to absolve themselves from guilt, their chauffeur-driven limousines making forays into the black crucible and leaving with trunks full of items of creativity they neither liked nor understood. At night the commercialism gave way to one element that has long been a source of strength—the crying sound of the guitar and the reverberations of the fender bass against the throb of drums sending a resonating message into the crowd, each listener lost in his own interpretation of the meaning. Morning brought the Junior Olympics, the element of competition rooted in the culture of the ghetto that has spawned the world's greatest athletes, now more formalized. Before there was a festival, you could see the Willie Mayses, the Hank Aarons, the Gayle Sayerses, and the Maury Willses practice after school on any vacant lot in the ghetto. It's the one class the ghetto child is never late for. Here the motivation comes not by birth but by cultural development and, for some, represents the only avenue of escape in the quest for dignity.

The grand finale was the parade, resplendent with vehicles generously supplied by the local Cadillac and Lincoln dealerships. It was also the day that few black politicians missed, their suits of mohair wool an awkward contrast to the polychromatic dashikis and caftan wraps that graced 103rd Street. As they sat astride the convertibles that moved through the masses, their faces revealed the insincerity of position, their eyes sweeping unfamiliar streets, and their ears echoing with somber responses from citizens who neither knew nor cared who they were. With frozen smiles, they played the game that would insure their reelection, even if they didn't know the boundaries of the constituency they represented.

Mathis's decision not to enter the school during the festival proved to be wise. There were several skirmishes between the police and residents of the projects during the week, the arid heat of the summer afternoon fanning the embers of provocation and antagonism. The 103rd Street Precinct doubled its nightly patrol along 103rd, and the fire department canceled all leaves. Ambulances made frequent runs past the school going to and from the Center, keeping the emergency room continually swamped. Residents of the projects moved freely through the streets, talking, joking, jiving, sometimes angrily, sometimes quietly, as they sought to escape the confinement and heat of poorly ventilated and inadequate housing.

Night brought little relief, but the darkness seemed to amplify the laughter of restless children and the profanities of their parents as they milled about the neighborhood in search of activity. Junkies huddled on the porch steps waiting for the pusher man with his pouch of white death and his suit of black velvet. Winos staggered back and forth across the street between the liquor stores and the projects, their booze-ridden bodies and anesthetized brains lurching from side to side as they fought to maintain their equilibrium. The barking of hungry dogs and the unrelenting cry of a newborn baby punctuated the blackness that veiled the ghetto, the glow of its sparsely placed street lights offering little more than street-sign identification on an isolated corner. The scream of terror from the victim of rape and the cry of orgasm were mixed with the sound of Stevie Wonder as they all blended together into a ghetto symphony.

Mathis spent each night in close proximity of the school, always on the lookout for something unusual. He saw nothing out of the ordinary, and, as the festival passed and the community began to settle back into the struggle, his vigil revealed no evidence to cast suspicion upon the school.

The director of Mafundi was more than cooperative, offering Mathis the use of the premises and the aid of employees who were desirous of volunteering. The first Wednesday after the festival brought only continued warm air from the gulf. A summer-league basketball game that evening at the school added to the inadvisability of carrying out the operation as planned. He decided to delay for an additional ten days in the hope of rain, but an urgent phone call from Carter changed that.

Arthur Shaw, the fifth member of the quintet that vandalized the school, was found strangled by the railroad tracks just south of Imperial Highway, his mutilated face unrecognizable. Mathis called for a meeting at Carter's and had full attendance by the time he arrived that evening. No one believed for a moment that Arthur's death was coincidental, it having become quite obvious that Buddy, Leon, and Damon would be next in line.

Leon was panic-stricken.

"I told you! I told you! These motherfuckers are crazy, man. They gonna kill all of us! Ain't nothin' we can do! Nothin'!" He sat on the edge of the couch facing the others, his eyes bulging with fear. He searched the room looking for a face that did not mirror his own anxiety but found only blank stares shielding equally grim thoughts.

Carter felt helpless. There was no absolute proof that the killings were in any way related to the incident at the school. Yet he had an ominous feeling that the connection was there, somewhere. He tried desperately to find words of reassurance, but his own suspicions betrayed his mask.

"One thing is sure: you can't go back home until this is over," he said.

Mathis was in full agreement, his face reflecting the concern that was Carter's. "I think they should stay here until something can be worked out for them to leave the city."

"Leave the city?" Damon said, his face distorted in dismay.

"Really!" said Leon with a cynical smile. "I ain't about to stay here and get myself killed—no, Lord!"

"Where you gonna go?" Buddy asked, his brow furrowed with curiosity.

"I mean, you just can't leave . . . without . . . I mean, you just *can't!*"

"Bullshit, you can't, baby!" Leon exclaimed. "Hey, I got relatives in Alabama; can't stand 'em, but I'll put up with 'em if it's necessary, for *days!*"

Carter picked up Mathis's suggestion and tossed it to Sable.

"Honey?"

He knew she would agree before she answered.

"We have an extra bedroom in the back. No problem. But how you gonna explain it to their parents?"

Carter had the answer. "How about if I send them all to the Big Apple for a few weeks? You know, sightseeing and all that."

"New York!" Mathis exclaimed, turning down the corners of his mouth as he raised his eyebrows in agreement. "You gonna pay their way?"

"Of course! What you think! Shouldn't be any difficulty with Damon, 'cause I know his mom. What do the rest of you think? Your folks go for it if I call and ask them personally? Don't have to tell them the real reason. Just say it's a community program for adolescents or something like that."

Carter's last statement amused Leon.

"You don't have to get *bourgeois,* Doc. Jus' say you helping the poor niggers in the ghetto see the world." He laughed as he spoke, pointing his finger in jest at Carter, who was seated precariously on the edge of the coffee table.

Carter managed a weak smile and shrugged his shoulders benignly.

"Buddy, what about it? Your folks go for it?"

"Yeah, if you call," he answered halfheartedly. He had missed the first meeting with Mathis and was not yet convinced that it was necessary to take such drastic measures. It would take the next few days to finally convince him that it would be in his best interest to join the group in New York.

Leon's fear disappeared momentarily as he began to exercise his fantasies.

"Man, I understand New York has some bitches whose nipples are as big as my thumb." He closed his fist and held up his thumb before his face, shaking his head from side to side.

"*Leon!*" exclaimed Sable from across the room in an acrimonious voice.

"Oh! Sorry, ma'am," he replied, placing his hand over his mouth and nose as his head bobbed to his smothered laugh.

With that out of the way, Mathis set about to alter his plans, the first allowance for weather.

"I think we should go this weekend, rain or not. No telling what might happen, especially if they have us fingered. You got a gun?" He directed his question to Carter, who didn't expect it.

"Who, me?" he asked, pointing at himself.

Mathis nodded his head.

"No! What the hell I need a *gun* for?" His all-too-familiar puzzled look graced his face again as he stared at Mathis.

"Just asked," said Mathis, yawning as he talked.

"I have one!" bellowed Sable, rising from her chair and disappearing into the bedroom.

Carter wheeled around in disbelief, his eyes fixed on the door behind him. "What do *you* mean you have a gun?" he shouted.

She reappeared in the room, her left hand holding a .25 Baretta automatic.

"Where the hell you get something like that, baby? You know how to use it?" His voice trailed off as she pulled out the clip and ejected a round from the chamber coolly. She handed the gun to Mathis, who inspected it closely and, in what would be her only lie to Carter, answered his question.

"No! Got it for self-protection, but never had to use it. Took up karate instead. Much easier."

"Doc," said Mathis as he returned the gun to Sable, "your old lady is a pistol—no pun intended!"

"No shit! Baby, where you keep that thing?"

"In a safe place," she said, smiling sheepishly. She had not meant to reveal this part of herself to Carter, but her intrigue with the unfolding events had compelled her to act impulsively. Now she would have to backtrack and cover the damage. Carter would be inquisitive—she knew that about him—but she felt she could smooth things over and give him the answers he wanted to hear. Unknown to him, she had always carried the Baretta in her tote bag wherever she went. She had believed in nonviolence when she was in Nashville, but the brutality she suffered at the hands of southern racists had caused her to insure that she would never allow it to happen again. She knew the risk of having an unlicensed weapon, but she had perfected the seduction in her smile and a mask of innocence, when stopped for traffic violations, that would assure her the freedom from being searched. She would have to be cautious now that the airlines were instituting the antihijack procedures, perhaps even to the point of switching to trains if necessary.

Carter was baffled. He had never seen this side of her personality, and it gave him an uneasy feeling. Other than the fact he loved her, he again realized how little he knew about her. They had talked at times about her past, and he knew what she had experienced, but not what it had done to her. He watched her as she slowly turned the gun over and over in her hands, the dull gray metal reflecting a broken image as the light caught her face. But why the gun? She had never impressed him as being constantly afraid. He would have to discuss it with her after the meeting.

"Well, I'll bring mine. Sable, you leave yours home, OK?" Mathis requested. She gave him her usual smile of agreement and returned to the bedroom.

"OK now, Saturday night—no!—make it Sunday night," Mathis continued. "Niggers be sleeping it off, trying to get it together for work Monday morning. Sunday night at eight. Everyone agree?"

"Hey baby, the ghetto don't *never* sleep!" Leon said forcefully. "Niggers out there got to *hustle*. They ain't gonna be 'sleep at no eight o'clock!"

"Yeah, I know, my man, but we just gonna meet first; choose the best time when it's quiet."

"Ain't *never* quiet in Watts," Leon said, his palm extended.

"Right on," Damon said, his hand slapping Leon's, the splitting sound echoing off the beamed ceiling.

Ignoring them, Mathis directed his comments to Carter. "We'll meet at Mafundi. Park in the lot in front of the entrance. The last karate class is over at nine, and we'll have it to ourselves after that."

Sable returned to the den and seated herself on the coffee table next to Carter, facing Mathis. She crossed her legs, and as she did so, her short skirt rode up on her thigh, exposing a good portion of her leggy frame. The sight was too much for Mathis; her shapely anatomy too distracting. He stood up, stretched, lit a cigarette, and walked to the other side of the room, seating himself on the divan that faced the sliding glass doors overlooking the pool. He continued, a stream of smoke pouring from his nose as he spoke.

"Carter, you stay at the Center until it's time, OK?"

"No problem!"

"Sable, you park in front of the Center between nine and ten, but don't get *out!* We'll be in constant touch by walkie-talkie. Understand?"

"Yeah, but why in front of the Center? That's a half block away from the school, and I can only see the front from there!"

"Right, it's a *natural!* If the pigs should stop and question why you're there, all you have to say is that you're waiting for someone who is being treated in the Center. Carter can have it set up in case they get pushy. But I'm betting the pigs won't be a problem. It'll be the brothers at that time of night most likely."

"Think you can handle that?" asked Carter.

"Really can! Besides, if the niggers get too carried away, I can always drive around the block—shit!"

"Both of you wear something comfortable, something casual. Doc, you and I have to wear sneakers. Got any?"

"Yeah," he replied, his thoughts still on the gun that Sable had produced. "You really think it's necessary to bring that gun?"

"Not necessary for you, but it is for me!"

"Why?"

"*Why?*" Mathis snapped. "Shit, Doc, don't know what's *down* there! I plan to give us every chance there is to get back in one piece." He hesitated, then said: "You know, the more I think about it, the more I think that *you* shouldn't go. Maybe I'd better do it alone. I think . . ."

"Oh bullshit, Mathis," Carter said, waving him silent. I was just *asking*. Of course I'm *going!*" He was trying hard to convince himself that there was no risk involved, but had little success. He shook with anticipation and trembled with fear the more Mathis talked. Before now the only dangerous thing he had ever faced was military maneuvers, and it was dangerous then only because he didn't know how to use the weapons. Why then did so simple a thing as breaking into a school bother him? He couldn't find an answer, and the more he thought about it, the more nervous he became. But it was Leon's question that bothered him the most.

"Why you wanna go through with this, Doc? I mean, you got a lot to lose if you get caught. I mean, you might find a junkie down there, and he blow you away just like he did Jimmie and Arthur!" Leon's eyes were expressive and full of conviction when he spoke. "Look here man, if I was you, an' had all this to lose"—he pointed toward the pool with his hand, then slowly looked about the room as if blessing it like a priest—"I'd really stay the hell out of there!"

He did have a lot to lose if they got caught. He refused to think of anything more serious happening. He was sure they were just blowing everything out of proportion. The idea of anyone getting killed over an elementary school seemed ridiculous. They should call the police and forget about it! But then, the more they talked, the more curious he was becoming.

"The kid's got a point, Doc! We get caught, that's breaking and entering, trespassing—the whole works! We probably get off with probation. I can stand it 'cause I ain't got nothin', but you can get put through the wringer for some shit like this. Might even get your license revoked or something like that. If it gets in the 'Black Dispatch,' the Center won't touch you with a ten-foot pole and you know it—right?"

He was right, as right could be. But there was a strange compulsion that seized him despite his fear. Yes, he was willing to risk this, all of this if necessary. He thought about his peers who sat perched high in their hillside habitats, involved in no meaningful activity outside the practice of medicine. None of them would ever be willing to risk a thing, but if something good came out of it they would be the first to complain that they should have been included.

Sable squeezed his hand affectionately, her chin resting on his shoulder as they talked among themselves, each expressing his own ideas about what should or shouldn't be done. Mathis interrupted the gab fest and ran down the rest of the plan. They would wait at Mafundi until some time after midnight and then make their move. It would be Sable's job to time the frequency of patrols by the Black and White and to relay reports on the traffic in and out of the Center. She would also monitor activity directly in front of the school, before and during the break-in.

"When was the last time you scaled a ten-foot fence, Doc?" Mathis asked casually, his feet propped on the ottoman.

"Do it every day, baby!" he answered facetiously. "I'm not in the same shape you are, but I'll give you a run for your money."

"Yeah, well you *will* get the chance, my man, this Sunday. You better practice jumping over that fence you got out there in that yard." He jerked his head in the direction of the glass doors as he talked. "You jump over *that* every day, and you be in as good a shape as me."

"Ha! Fat chance," said Carter glibly.

"Oh! I almost forgot. Bring a flashlight, preferably a five-cell job if you got one. I don't plan to turn on no lights!" He spoke very slowly and distinctly, enunciating each word and gesturing dramatically with his hands as he made each point. "If whatever or whoever it is, wherever it is, can't be seen with a flashlight, then it ain't going to be seen—period!"

Sable yawned loudly and Mathis picked up the hint, rising to his feet while struggling to keep his balance on legs that had gone numb.

"Oh, yeah! One last thing," Mathis said as he reached the door, still trying to limber up his extremities. "Be sure to wear something dark that evening."

"Jesus Christ, Mathis! You sound like the honkies on television: got to wear something dark so we can blend in with the night," he whispered loudly, cloak-and-dagger style. "Shit, man, we already *black*. Why wear something the same color you already are?"

Mathis smiled, his body half out of the door. "I'll be in touch," he said, disappearing behind the sound of the teak-wood door as it swung shut.

"That nigger is crazy! Ain't got a brain in his skull," Carter said as he moved to help Sable clear the coffee table of ash trays and empty glasses.

"You having second thoughts, baby?" she asked, still sensing his uncertainty.

Carter wanted to say yes. He wanted to tell her how scared he was, how unused he was to this kind of stress. But his pride muffled his thoughts, so he told her what she wanted to hear.

"Naw, just concerned about everyone. Sure would like to know what *is* in the basement. I'm inclined to agree with Mathis—whatever it is, if anything, is either very big or very small." He paused for a moment, pondering a fleeting thought that flashed to his mind.

Sable noticed and responded. "Penny for your thoughts."

"Just thinking about that other kid that was killed. Strange that he should be connected with this. Sure gives you an eerie feeling, doesn't it?"

"I dunno, guess so," she said. It did not bother her that there might be some danger. She had lived through danger for days on end and survived. She would never be able to tell him the whole truth about herself, about the gun. She had been trained well in its use, and it had become a part of her. She would not hesitate to use it when necessary. Violence did not impinge upon her nature, and although she had a tremendous passion for the humanity of others, she did not intend to let anything stand in the way of fulfilling her own needs. Carter was one of those needs now, but if they were about to get into something of any magnitude, then she'd just as soon not have him involved. She knew he really wasn't the type for anything but a bourgeois existence, except he had a little more compassion and sensitivity for other black folks than most. He was honest and trusting; perhaps too much so.

The next day Carter made arrangements in New York for the boys to stay with relatives and booked reservations on an American Airlines flight leaving Sunday afternoon. The remainder of the week seemed to move at a snail's pace. While Carter didn't jump any fences, he did start jogging daily at a nearby high school athletic field. He soon found out how much he was out of shape, the twelve years of easy military life having taken its toll on his physical ability. As the weekend approached, he found it necessary to take a Valium at night to calm his nerves. The anxiety was mounting, and while he tried desperately to suppress it, he had little success. His nights were restless, his days irritated. He had little appetite and lost three pounds. At work he found his concentration impaired and his diagnostic acumen faulty. One of the nurses asked if he was ill. He started to call Mathis several times to say he couldn't go through with it, but each time changed his mind at the last instant, having convinced himself that the whole thing was ridiculous to begin with.

At grand rounds Friday morning he was so ill-prepared that the senior staff physician suggested that he might want to wait and present his cases the following week, after he had taken care of his personal problems. Carter was embarrassed but complied, leaving the Center early to be by himself. He spent the afternoon on Pacific Coast Highway just north of Malibu, the black Ferrari an intimate companion on the picturesque but lonely mountain road. He returned at eight, had dinner, and watched "Marcus Welby, M.D.," on TV before retiring. He spent Saturday around the house doing nothing but odd jobs for Sable. The boys spent all of their time in the pool, oblivious of the events soon to follow. They indulged their fantasies to the fullest extent possible, fantasies that heretofore had only been elusive dreams carved from a kaleidoscope of multicolored billboards, Hollywood movies, and General Motors automobiles.

Sunday morning broke like a glass against the floor, the brilliant fractured rays of sunlight piercing dark cumulous clouds that covered the sky like a troop formation. As the void of sleep began to leave him, he could feel Sable's warm breath gently caress the back of his neck, and her soft brown legs entwined in his. Her arm was limp across his waist, and as he slowly turned to face her slumbering body, he felt the nipples of her breasts as they brushed against the fabric of his skin.

She stirred momentarily at his change in position and then returned to quiescence, her fluffy natural all but invisible beneath the covers. Like Siamese twins, they always slept touching one another throughout the night, having become so accustomed to each other that even deep in sleep the absence of the other produced discomfort.

Carter had awakened spontaneously, his system so tense that he found it difficult just to lie awake next to Sable, something he always did on Sunday mornings. They would often lounge around the house together—touching, feeling, and enjoying each other's presence—but not today. As per agreement with Mathis he would be at the Center until the evening. It was unusual for him to come into the Center on Sunday unless he had a patient that needed checking, but the emergency staff welcomed his presence and thought nothing strange about his willingness to help out for an extra shift.

Sable would arrange to take the three youngsters to the airport in time for their flight. Because of a delay due to mechanical difficulties, they would be leaving much later than originally scheduled, giving Sable just enough time to return home and eat before leaving to meet the others at the school.

At seven-forty-five Carter excused himself from duty in the emergency room and left the Center for Mafundi, one block away. To his surprise, it had begun to sprinkle, the sky giving an ominous warning of future turbulence. He walked briskly to his car parked in front of the emergency entrance, and drove to Mafundi, arriving some ten minutes after Mathis, who sat silently watching a karate match between two youngsters, both under ten. Carter joined him on the edge of the mat and fixed his eyes on the movements of the two combatants in the center.

Young and untrained, they grappled with each other, their arms and legs flailing with abandon as they moved about the mat in awkward fashion. Mathis attended the training sessions regularly and knew that in a year the same two would be coordinated and deft in their movements, their actions much more precise and their stances secure. The martial arts had swept the country much like ten-speed bicycles, but, with the exception of Mafundi, ghetto youth had little chance to learn the discipline.

Mathis continued to watch the match, unaware that Carter was seated next to him, until it ended and his concentration was turned to others in the room.

"Say, hey," he said, imitating Willie Mays's commercial voice. "Glad you could make it."

"No kidding? I didn't know you cared. How long you been here?"

"Ten—fifteen minutes, I guess. I always come here on Sundays to watch the karate sessions." Not an expert, he had spent considerable time learning the martial arts while in the army, although he had never perfected his skill. He might have become quite proficient if the army had given him half a chance. He cursed to himself as the memory crossed his mind, the stinging bitterness welling up in him as he fought to contain its expression.

"You know, it's beginning to rain, man," said Carter, gesturing toward the window to the side of them.

"Seriously? Out of sight! Just what the doctor ordered. I was wondering all day whether or not it would happen. Hey look, that makes it much easier for us now and—" He paused, his hand pulling the gold curtain to one side as he peered out of the window at the sidewalk, its slate-gray appearance now becoming reflective as the rain covered its surface. He continued: "And we'll need all the cover we can get!"

Carter joined him at the window, his dark brown turtle-neck sweater and faded Levi's contrasting sharply to the blue jumpsuit worn by Mathis. They stared together for a moment, until interrupted by the clapping of hands indicating the start of the next match. They returned to the periphery and remained until the session had finished.

The community volunteers served refreshments to the participants and onlookers as the milling crowd of youthful black faces imitated the positions and sounds of the martial arts while stuffing cookies and doughnuts into their mouths to stem the tide of hunger that was their constant companion.

Mathis introduced Carter to the director of Mafundi and then returned to the window that faced the school. He remained motionless and only once left his position to get a cup of coffee, returning in time to catch a fleeting glance of the blue Pinto as Sable crossed Wilmington Avenue, heading toward the Center.

He motioned for Carter across the room to join him.

"As soon as these kids get out of here I'll bring the walkie-talkies in. I saw Sable drive by a minute ago. I'm sure she's parked by now."

"How's she gonna get a walkie-talkie?" Carter asked.

"She's already got one. I brought it by the pad; showed her how to use it and all that on Friday."

"Cool," Carter said and looked around the room. The crowd was beginning to thin now, the last of the youngsters making a mad dash across the parking lot to a waiting car blocking the driveway. He looked at his watch. It was nine-fifty, and Sable expected a call by ten. Without speaking, he nudged Mathis and pointed to the luminous dial. He heard the door slam for the last time and watched the director disappear down 103rd Street toward the tracks.

It was quiet. They were alone and it was time.

Mafundi stood silent like a majestic castle, its darkened interior akin to a mausoleum. It was about to launch an investigation that would lead to the most frightening discovery in the history of black America. Its role would go unannounced and unpublicized, but it would fulfill its destiny in a way that even its founders would never have imagined.

CHAPTER 9

IT WAS RAINING steadily now, the sound of the cascading water creating an echo as it fell against the concrete beneath the alcove shielding the entrance to Mafundi. The sound of Sable's voice broke the silence as it burst through the crackling static of the walkie-talkie.

"Hello! Hello! This is position one calling position two, do you read me? Over!" She repeated it two more times and then waited for a reply.

"Loud and clear position one, this is position two. How do you read?" Mathis's voice was confident and authoritative, his diction clear and smooth.

Sable reported sparse traffic going to and from the Center. A church service had recently let out, and there were still a few people standing on the steps waiting for transportation. Other than that it was quiet. She had parked in front of the Center as planned and as close to the corner of Grape Street as possible. From there, she could see down 103rd Street, past the school and as far as Wilmington Avenue. She had a clear view of both sides of the street in either direction. The stores directly across from the school were closed, and the street lamp at the corner of 103rd and Grape was out. That, plus the rain, gave them every possible advantage.

"We going now?" asked Carter nervously.

"Not yet. It's too early. I'm going to sit on it for another hour and gamble that the rain holds." There was a twinge of doubt in his voice. Carter could not see his face in the dark, only the shadow of his form as he moved back and forth in front of the window.

"Let's look at the diagram now. I want to make absolutely sure we know where the hell we're going."

They moved to the back of the building where a small utility closet was located. It was cramped but fully enclosed and would not emit the light into the rest of the building.

Mathis switched off his flashlight as he turned on the closet light that hung overhead. He oriented himself on the diagram and began to show Carter where they would enter the school, the approximate distances, and the location of the basement.

They would have to get over the fence initially, stay close to the building until they were in back of it, then force the door with a crowbar. Damon had assured them that it was easy to do, but that was calculated on the assumption that the door had not been fixed. If it took more than five minutes, or if a new lock had been installed, they would have to abort the operation until the proper tools could be obtained. They would know soon enough. Mathis glanced at his watch, then back to the diagram, his fingers tracing once again the outline of the path they were to take.

Carter could feel the pounding in his chest. He felt for his pulse but withdrew his hand when he noticed Mathis looking at him. He wanted to walk out and forget the whole thing, but each time he tried to speak something blocked the words. He thought of his home, his car, his friends, and Sable. What if something were to go wrong? What if they were caught? What if they were underworld people involved? They might be heading into a trap! He had to get out of it somehow! He had too much to lose. Leon was right! He should have stayed the hell away from there!

They returned to the front of the building, positioned themselves in front of the window, and observed the infrequent traffic en route to the projects, the rain creating a prismatic effect against the reflected glare of the occasional headlights.

They exchanged few words during the next hour and a half, Mathis totally immersed in his concern for the prevailing weather. Carter paced nervously in the dark, his hands cold from apprehension, his legs weak from fear.

"Say look, Mathis, I . . . ," he blurted out compulsively, his thoughts on the tip of his tongue.

Mathis picked up the hesitation and, without turning around, answered in an expectant but inquiring manner: "Yes?"

Carter was blank. He knew what he wanted to say, but the words wouldn't form in his throat. He was already committed. He knew it, and Mathis knew it, but Mathis would spare him the embarrassment of admitting his fear openly. He chose to neutralize Carter with a question of his own. It worked.

"What time you got?" Carter took a deep breath and sighed. Relieved that his train of thought was interrupted, he glanced at the dial on the Omega, its luminous glow returning the stare in silence.

"Twelve-fifteen," he said.

Sable's voice scratched through the speaker of the walkie-talkie, relieving the tension between them.

"Hello position two, this is position one. Do you read me? Over!"

"Position one, this is position two. Go ahead."

"All is quiet in the ghetto. A hundred and third Street is clear down to the high school to the east and as far as I can see to the west. The rain is moderate but appears steady—over!"

Mathis looked out the window once again before answering and, having satisfied himself of her accuracy, responded.

"Position one, this is position two; we're rolling! Will advise you of our movements as we make them. Out!"

"This is it, Doc. Time to go!" He collapsed the antenna on the walkie-talkie and, with eyes now accustomed to the dark, headed toward the faint light cast by the window next to the door.

"From now on, we whisper, understand? And no flashlights unless it's necessary!"

"Right on," said Carter, following Mathis closely as they headed out into the rain. It wasn't raining heavily, but enough to have the effect that Mathis had hoped for—black folks were staying inside!

They walked briskly in tandem across Wilmington first and then over to the Shell station on the opposite side of 103rd Street. Mathis's movements were like a cat's, quick and precise. He stayed close to the shops that lined the streets, changing his pace at will whenever suspicious of the next step or the next building. Quietly, the two darkly clad forms, obscured by the rain, moved down 103rd Street toward the front of the school. The chain-link fence that bordered the playground passed them to the left, the obnoxious clanging of an unsecured tetherball chain swinging in the slight breeze the only sound heard above the rain.

As they approached Anzac Street, Mathis slowed, his left hand motioning for Carter to do the same. They moved quickly around the corner and flattened themselves against the side of a building, looking in both directions for the element of security. They were directly in front of the school now, the classroom building only twenty-five to thirty yards away. The chain-link fence ended at the classroom building and, for some unknown reason, did not seem as high as the rest of the fence. Nonetheless, it was a formidable obstacle to overcome.

Mathis extended the antenna of the walkie-talkie and advised Sable of their location. There was a moment of silence before she answered: "103rd Street is clear." He collapsed the antenna, attached the instrument to his belt, and motioned for Carter to move closer to him.

"I'm going over first and check the back. If it's clear I'll flash once, and you'll follow. If it's not, I'll return. If I don't do either one, you get the hell *out* of here!" He punched Carter on the shoulder and then moved in front of him in the direction of the school.

Mathis was in excellent physical condition and gained momentum as he started across the street. By the time he was at the curb, he was going at full speed, springing two-thirds of the way up the fence and vaulting his body over the remainder. He landed on both feet without losing balance and quickly disappeared behind the front building. The rattle of the fence subsided, and the street was quiet once again. Twenty seconds later Carter saw the beam from his flashlight motion up and down and then cut off.

Carter started across the street, but his steps were clumsy and his timing off. He reached for the fence but found himself no more than a few feet off the ground. He clambered and muscled his way to the top, dropping awkwardly to the ground in spread-eagle fashion. He joined Mathis behind the building as they both silently waited for the noise to abate. Carter, exhausted and breathing heavily, wiped the rain from his eyes that obscured his vision and turned to Mathis to speak, but he waved him silent, his finger over his lips. They moved to a small recess in the building where the trash bins were kept. Mathis contacted Sable on the walkie-talkie; it was still clear on 103rd Street.

They moved to the rear of the classroom building and observed the entire schoolyard through the mist of the rain. The playground was beginning to flood, necessitating a slight detour from their planned path to the door in the rear of the building.

The door was as Damon said it would be: steel, poorly constructed, and sitting approximately one-half to three-quarters of an inch off the molding, but, even more important, there was no additional lock or security mechanism. Mathis studied the lock momentarily and then pulled a small bar from under his pants leg, where he had kept it strapped to his calf, and began to force the lock mechanism with a prying motion. Almost without effort and in what seemed like seconds, he was able to move the catch mechanism far enough so that the door swung open. It did so under its own power, exposing the steps that led into the blackness below.

Mathis looked at Carter for a moment, an intriguing smile on his face. He replaced the bar on his calf and motioned for Carter to follow him inside. They closed the door behind them, trying the knob several times to make certain it would open from the inside. Satisfied that it would, Mathis closed the door for the last time, leaving them momentarily in darkness until the piercing shaft of light from his flashlight illuminated the stairwell, casting grotesque shadows against the walls before them.

Mathis pulled out the antenna of the walkie-talkie and contacted Sable again. Her voice was clear but weak, necessitating an increase in the volume whenever she talked. They would stay in constant communication now that they were in the school, and she was to report any activity that took place within the proximity of their location. They were to contact her if any untoward situation occurred during their search of the basement. The plan was to spend thirty minutes or less before returning to the street unless the situation warranted an extension.

According to the diagram, the steps leading to the basement divided at the first level, their present position. One set led to the door they had just entered, and the other descended to the utility section. Mathis guessed it was a relatively new school, built in the late sixties. Steel guard rails replaced wooden banisters while concrete and brick eliminated planking and plasterboard. The walls were painted a light green and were traversed with various pipes of different sizes.

As they moved down the stairs, Carter noticed for the first time the strange silence that surrounded them, the noise of the rain muffled by the roof three floors above. The stairs ended directly opposite a door marked: AUTHORIZED PERSONS ONLY. It was closed but unlocked. Cautiously Mathis pushed it open, the large hinges squeaking only momentarily.

They entered a large congested basement area that obviously lived up to its name. Sinks, boilers, and electrical generators occupied most of the space; the remaining contents were portable, and could be moved in and out at will when necessary. Since the basement was fairly large, Carter suggested that they divide it in half, each searching a section at a time so as not to miss anything. Mathis agreed and took the section closest to the entrance.

They searched thoroughly each closet, each recess, each alcove. They explored beneath each boiler and generator, emptied every bucket, scrutinized every shelf, and opened every electrical panel. Sable's voice broke the silence intermittently to report the passing of a car or the leaving of an ambulance. It was still raining, and by and large the streets were empty as the ghetto slept, trying to gather strength for a Monday morning that would bring with it little more than all the Mondays preceding it for the past three hundred years.

"What time you got?" Mathis asked.

Carter checked the luminous dial on his wrist.

"Ten after one."

"Ain't nothin' down here, man. Let's get the fuck up to the street!"

"Right on, baby."

They returned to the door, Mathis sweeping the room one last time with the beam from his flashlight. Suddenly, out of the corner of his eye, Carter caught a glimpse of reflected light off the wall behind one of the boilers.

"Do that again!" he said excitedly.

"Shh, not so much *noise!* Do what again, Doc?" Mathis asked.

"With your flashlight! *Look* . . . "

"You mean like *this?*" he said, moving the light in the same general direction as before, only slower.

"Yeah, yeah, that's it. Look over to your right. See it?"

Mathis repeated the motion several times until the light fell on the spot Carter had seen.

"Now I do. What is it, a piece of metal or something?"

They moved toward the source of the reflection, both flashlights trained on the wall that now intrigued them. As they moved to the side of the boiler, the glistening object revealed itself to be a small handlelike structure protruding from the wall. They scrutinized the surrounding wall carefully, and only then did the significance of the metal object become apparent—it was a door! It was small, only four and a half to five feet high by Mathis's estimation. He guessed the width at nineteen to twenty inches. The outline of the door was skillfully blended with the wall, and, had not the handle reflected when hit by the light, they would have missed it. Mathis reached up to grasp the handle and gave it a slight tug. Because of the proximity of the boiler there was relatively little room in which to maneuver for the best leverage. He tried it again, this time bracing his foot against the wall itself. It worked, the outline of the door clearly visible as it moved away from the wall.

"Call Sable and let her know what's happening, will you?" said Mathis, still working on the mechanics of the door.

"Position one, this is position two—over!" Carter began.

"Position two, this is position one; go ahead—over!"

"Looks like we got something, a door of some kind. We almost missed it! We're gonna stay a while longer—over!"

"Be *careful*—over!" Sable's voice amplified through the speaker.

By now Mathis had moved the heavy steel door as far as he could, the large boiler blocking any further movement. The opening was narrow but would allow passage of one person at a time without difficulty. Mathis checked the time on his watch and then unzipped the top of his jumpsuit, removing a .32-caliber revolver from his shoulder holster. He released the safety, advanced a shell into the chamber, and moved cautiously toward the darkened opening, his flashlight waving from side to side as he sought to minimize any risk before entering.

He turned to Carter and spoke; his voice was subdued and confident: "Well, this is what it's all about. You ready?"

"As I'll ever be!" For the past thirty minutes Carter had completely forgotten his fear. He was like a driver before a race or an athlete before a game; the anticipation builds up to a thundering crescendo only to be dissipated by the fall of the flag or the sound of the whistle, as each competitor becomes solely preoccupied with the task before him. So it was with Carter who, only moments before, had been troubled by his doubts in face of apprehension. Now intrigued by the discovery, his anxiety had been relegated to lesser status. Curiosity was now predominant.

They stooped as they moved through the entranceway into the void of darkness, broken only by the two beams of light that sought to define its limits. They found themselves in what appeared to be a small anteroom some eight to ten feet high and equally wide. They faced a door that was of conventional size, and, like the door that opened from the playground, it stood almost half an inch off the molding. While Mathis tried the knob, Carter scanned the room with his light, its concrete walls bare and sterile.

"Aw, *shit!* Look at that, Mathis!" he said, directing his attention to the ceiling above the door. A small closed-circuit camera mounted on a platform stared at them from the corner to their right.

"Don't touch anything!" Mathis said. "It must be infrared because . . . no it's not—*look!*" He pointed to the recessed lights in the ceiling directly above the door. "Light switch must be in there," he said, gesturing with his flashlight at the door.

"Is it on?" Carter asked, concerned.

"What? The camera? Can't tell, but I doubt it. Not unless it's infrared or something." Mathis took one more scan with his flashlight, then turned his attention back on the door. He tried the knob once again, tucking the flashlight under his arm to free his hand. With minimal effort the door swung free of its catch, releasing a stale, fetid atmosphere into the anteroom.

"God*damn*, that shit smells foul!" said Carter, clamping his nose in disdain.

Mathis opened the door to its full width and, as cautiously as before, moved once again into the blackness beyond. The smell was nauseating. Mathis had to take several deep breaths to abort regurgitation.

Once past the door, their lights defined an officelike structure, fully glass enclosed except for a door in the middle. It had desks, chair, telephones, typewriters, file cabinets, and lamps. Carter swept his finger along the top of one of the desks and wiped the dust on his pants.

"Hey, look at this, Carter!" exclaimed Mathis excitedly, waving his flashlight toward an elongated cabinet structure with glass-enclosed door panels. Mathis opened one of the panels to avoid the reflected light from the glass.

"I don't see nothin'," said Carter, peering into the empty space.

"Look at it again," said Mathis insistently, his flashlight making eerie shadows on the walls about them.

"I don't see any . . . uh, oh! Yes, I see it now. A gun rack?"

Mathis nodded his head in agreement and closed the panel door. On each side of the office, was mounted a small camera in much the same fashion as in the anteroom. To the left was a bathroom and, next to it, a small kitchen facility. Carter spotted a metal panel flush against the wall adjacent to the door that led to the anteroom. He brought it to Mathis's attention.

"Hey, man! Look here; probably the fuse box, huh?" His flashlight outlined its periphery.

"Yeah, probably, but don't touch anything!" repeated Mathis emphatically.

Because of the reflection from the glass, they were unable to see beyond the office.

"Looks like some kind of bomb shelter, huh?" questioned Carter.

"Can't tell just yet. Let's see what's on the other side of the glass," suggested Mathis, compulsively checking the safety of his .32 automatic. "I don't know what all this shit means, but I got a feeling the answer's through that door."

For the third time in as many minutes they moved through a doorway that led to the unknown. The presence of the gun rack had started each of them thinking, and although neither verbalized it, they had developed identical thoughts. It would remain for them to see beyond the glass to confirm their suspicions.

Once out of the office they found themselves at the junction of two corridors branching off from each other in a V shape. They extended beyond the range of their flashlights, necessitating their having to walk the entire distance. The floors were of tile, thick with dust and dirt. The ceilings were twelve to fifteen feet high and covered with acoustical tile. Long fluorescent lights hung suspended from the ceiling like stalactites in a cave. As their flashlights moved from side to side, they projected latticed shadows against the concrete walls that formed the rear of rooms enclosed by cages of steel.

Mathis stopped midway down the first corridor and knelt on one knee, his chin supported by the palm of his hand, his elbow resting at mid-thigh. He stared blankly at the cells to either side of the corridor, their empty cots and porcelain toilets beckoning a grim memory of a long-forgotten experience as a ghetto youth, shut off from society like an animal stripped of its freedom to exist in its own natural habitat. He could no longer contain his anger.

"A prison! It's a goddamn prison! Can you believe this shit? A motherfucking *jail*—right here in the community under the motherfucking *school!* I can't believe it! A goddamn concentration camp!"

Carter was equally dumbfounded. So this was why they were killed! Jimmie must have accidentally discovered the door. No wonder someone wanted him out of the way. But who?

They continued to walk the length of the corridor, their flashlights searching cells at random for some clue to explain the reason for its existence. It was difficult to determine the size of the facility, but Mathis guessed from the location that it ran beneath the entire expanse of the playground. Both corridors were identical, each one containing a hundred and twenty cells. Every cell had two cots, a single toilet, and a wash bowl. There were no windows, vents, or doors between the cells, only the one hinged door that opened into

124

the corridor. At the far end of each corridor there was a self-contained kitchen with two ovens, a sink, a large freezer, and several cupboards.

Next to the office structure and at the front of the left corridor was what appeared to be a small dispensary. It had two examining rooms, a locked medicine cabinet, and outlets on the walls for oxygen, electricity, suction, otoscope, and receptor plugs for cardiac monitors.

"Position two, this is position one. Come in *please!*" Sable's voice interrupted their concentration and reminded them of her concern for such a long pause between communications.

"Position one, this is position two; we hit the jackpot. Coming out in five—over!"

"Roger." The hissing of the walkie-talkie fell silent as the men continued the exploration of the facility. It was quite apparent that it had never been occupied. The mattresses were still wrapped, the lighting fixtures were taped, and the locks on the cell doors still contained keys enclosed in plastic. In each corner of the corridor, close to the ceiling, the cameras stood poised on their pedestals, observing anything in their paths. Carter noticed one curious difference, however, in the platform that supported the camera mounted above the office facing both corridors.

"What's that?" he asked, his flashlight bathing the camera in light.

Mathis examined the camera critically and then commented: "It's on a tripod!"

"A tripod! What's so special about that?"

"Means it moves, that's what!"

"So what controls the movement?" Carter asked, not really expecting an answer. But before Mathis could speak, a thought entered his mind so convincingly that he blurted it out loudly.

"The panel! I bet it's the panel!"

"What are you talking about?"

But Carter had already started for the office and didn't hear Mathis's question. He motioned for him to follow with his flashlight. By the time Mathis figured out what Carter was up to, he had already reached the door and was tugging at the steel ring connected to the panel that was next to it.

"Hey, wait a minute!" Mathis shouted, forgetting his edict about whispering. "Don't touch any . . ."

The sound of the spring vibrating as it broke free of its catch cut him off in midsentence. He joined Carter as he opened the small metal door and looked at the maze of electrical instruments that occupied the space. The fuse box was on a tall wooden board that was supported by hinges. Carter reached in and slowly pulled the fuse box toward him, exposing a large recess behind it. On the bottom shelf of the recess was a videotape machine, its half-inch tape approximately two-thirds wound. Above the machine and mounted flush with the fuse box was a large clock with sophisticated armatures, its wiring connected to an outlet that received wiring from the videotape machine.

"Well, I'll be goddamned! Ain't that a bitch! The motherfucker's on a timer. That's how this whole damn *place* works. What made you think to look here?"

Carter couldn't really answer him because he didn't know himself. It was just a spontaneous idea, an impulse, a hunch he followed.

The timer was set to trip the master light switch and the videotape machine simultaneously every hour for one minute. Although it was not evident, he correctly guessed that a series of relays fed a picture from each camera in the facility into the videotape in a prearranged order, thus assuring that nothing would escape detection.

Closer scrutiny also told them that they had about two minutes before it would be activated.

"Let's get the fuck out of here, Doc!" said Mathis, closing the panel door quickly.

"I'm right behind you, baby. Move it!"

Without hesitation the two men moved briskly through the door that led to the anteroom, their shadows dancing against the walls in magnified pseudo-ritualistic fashion. Mathis closed the door to the office and followed Carter through the entranceway back into the basement of the school. They managed to close the door flush with the wall just as the light in the anteroom crept through the space between the ground and the bottom of the door.

"Cut your light off, Doc," said Mathis, breathing heavily as he leaned against the boiler facing the wall. They stared at the dim strip of light beneath the door until it vanished, their flashlights once again cutting through the gloom that surrounded them.

"Baby, that was *close!* I'm sure that's the only way the kid found this place." Mathis, waving his flashlight at the base of the door, continued: "Probably saw the light and figured there had to be a door here somewhere. Wouldn't take a whole lot of doing to find it. More than likely he didn't realize the cameras were on him. Too bad!"

Carter rubbed his tired eyes and suggested they get back to the street. Mathis agreed, and they notified Sable. She was relieved for several reasons.

The rain was beginning to ease up, and the Black and White had made more than one pass down 103rd Street. They would have to be cautious on leaving. Carter checked his watch—2:00 A.M. They had spent nearly an hour in the basement and discovered something, the implications of which might mean a lot of trouble for a lot of people.

They moved to the stairwell and exited onto the playground, inching their way back around toward the front of the school to position themselves across from Anzac Street. Sable kept constant surveillance on the activity around them and, when she felt it was safe, cleared them over the fence.

They returned to Mafundi as they had left, cautiously and quietly. Sable joined them in the parking lot to pick up Mathis, who had left his car at home. They drove to the house in silence and at three-thirty found themselves seated before the fireplace, the aroma of Maxwell House once again filling their nostrils as they prepared to reconstruct the events of the evening. The fire before them held their attention in hypnotic convenience; fatigue combined with disbelief preoccupied their thoughts.

CHAPTER 10

"**W**ELL?" SAID SABLE, sitting receptively on the ottoman next to the marble fireplace, its walls licked by the dancing flames from the burning logs.

"Well, what?" Carter swiveled slowly around in the chair, his fingers tapping nervously on the armrest.

"So what's the deep, dark secret? What did you find? You've been acting like you saw a tomb of death or something!"

Mathis looked at Carter for a moment, smiling bitterly. He stood up to stretch, his long brown arms grasping at thin air as he tried to squeeze the fatigue from his muscles.

"Don't everybody speak at once," persisted Sable. She sipped her coffee, placed the cup on the table, and turned her attention to Carter, still revolving in the chair, his eyes staring blankly ahead.

"Baby? What's going on?"

"A jail," he said. He took a deep breath, held it, looked at Sable, and rubbed his eyes, speaking as he exhaled. "We found a jail under the school. Ain't never been used. Full of dirt and shit, but wouldn't take nothin' to put it in order."

Sable, her eyes squinting, moved to the edge of the ottoman and looked at Carter intently. "You found a what?" she said, not wanting to believe what she had heard. But the look on his face convinced her he was serious.

She threw it to Mathis for confirmation.

"Mathis?"

"He's right, baby! That's what we found—a jail," he said, standing in front of the sliding glass doors that faced the pool.

"A *jail!* You really found a jail?" she said, trying to convince herself now.

Carter cleared the air. "It's a concentration camp, honey," he said with an air of authority.

"A concentration camp? Like they had in Germany?" she asked, startled.

"Exactly," Carter replied.

They described the facility to her in detail, and as they spoke, each taking turns to add his version, a metamorphosis overtook them as their shock gave way to vehement anger. Mathis was more visibly disturbed.

"Those motherfucking honkies got the nerve to build a goddamn concentration camp underneath the school. Can you *imagine* that shit! Do you know what that means? Do you really know what that means? It means that anytime there's a disturbance, the man can put five hundred niggers . . ."

"Five hundred?" Carter interrupted. "How do you know it'll hold five hundred?"

" 'Cause there's a hundred and twenty cells in each corridor, right? And there's two beds in each cell. . . ." Carter waved him silent, nodding his head in agreement. Mathis continued.

"The man can put five hundred niggers down there and hold them incommunicado forever! Niggers *never* get the fuck out of there!"

"I thought it was illegal to have concentration camps in this country."

"Sable," said Mathis, his eyes spitting disgust as he looked at her anguished face, "don't you know, baby, that the man *makes* the laws? Shit, he don't have to *obey* 'em. That's just for *niggers* to do—shit!

"But under a *school*, of all places. Look! Do you have any doubt now that there ain't nothin' planned for niggers except genocide? Do you have *any* doubt? Huh?"

Sable stared at the fire in silence for a moment, her half-empty cup now cold. She shook her head and, with her arms clasped tightly around her chest, rocked slowly back and forth, the crackling of the fire offering little consolation to her thoughts.

They sat in silence for a long time, each lost in thoughts of helplessness. They had gone searching for a clue to murder but never expected to find anything of this magnitude. Carter was the first one to say it!

"No wonder they killed the kids. Jimmie found it. Probably figured that the rest of 'em knew about it, too. That's some *deep* shit, man!"

"Not as deep as it's gonna *get*, though. Whole *lotta* folks gonna get hurt behind this."

"How you mean, baby?" Carter asked.

Sable continued angrily. "Just wait till the community gets word of this. They will . . ."

"We ain't gonna *tell* the community," said Mathis convincingly. "Don't you see, baby, if we let this out of the bag, niggers will go off, man, I mean really *off!* That's all the man needs to get the shit started. He would *love* to put that jail to use, just love it! Wouldn't waste any time getting his law-and-order forces mobilized. Shit, Watts would be an armed camp—not that it isn't now—but they'd be hauling niggers off to jail by the truckload."

"Well, who we going to tell?" Sable asked, her voice becoming hoarse. She cleared her throat and repeated the question.

"Sure as hell ain't gonna tell the politicians," Mathis said, half-laughing as he spoke. "Can you see some proper Negro gettin' on TV an' talkin' 'bout how sure he is that there is no malice intended on the part of the government? Shit. Those niggers' the worst ones to tell *any*thing to—shit! All they'd do is make a political football out of it, call for investigations, commissions, and all that bullshit!" Mathis had a particular distrust of politicians that stemmed from his experience with the military. He had solicited their help during his court-martial, but none would commit themselves, claiming prior obligations when in reality they were afraid of making public statements that would endanger their political positions.

"And we really can't tell the cops, 'cause *they* probably in on it."

"Yeah, I hadn't thought of that. This is some funky shit, huh?"

"Really!"

"So if we ain't going to tell anyone, what good is knowing to us?" Sable, always the inquisitive one, continued to play the role of the devil's advocate. "I mean, after all, what can we do about it by ourselves?" she said, her voice straining.

"Well, for one thing, we need more information," said Mathis, pacing the floor with his hands in his hip pockets. "We need to know who built it, how it was built, when it was built, why it was built, who the contractor was, who the architects were—you see? We need all that information *before* we worry about what we gonna do about it!" Mathis became more worked up as he talked. Beads of sweat formed on his forehead as he gestured convincingly with his hands, his voice a monotonous nasal pitch that resonated with each word.

"Who the hell is going to give us information like that, the mayor?" said Carter facetiously, filing his nails with an emory board.

"We have to get it ourselves, obviously!"

"How?"

"Simple. There are two ways to go about it. Architects and contractors for a public project, such as the school, have to bid. Right?"

He searched their faces for agreement, and, when they nodded, he continued. "OK, so since they have to bid for the contract, the bids are a matter of the public record, right? Now those records are available at the Hall of Records downtown, so all you have to do is request to see them." He stood on his tiptoes, supremely confident, smiling as if he had just enlightened a class of children and expecting to be held in awe for his words of wisdom.

"And the second way?" asked Sable, her voice reduced to a whisper.

"Well . . ." Mathis paused, lighting a cigarette. He stared momentarily at the burning flame as if hypnotized. His thoughts organized, he extinguished the match and continued: "We still need to know how it was built. I mean, what kind of materials were used and what kind of electrical system and . . ."

"But doesn't all that information come from the contractor?" asked Carter.

"Yeah, but what the contractor says he uses and what he *really* uses to cut costs are two different things. Besides, I want to know who supplied all this stuff."

"What good is all that going to do us?"

"You can't go around blowing off about things unless you got your shit together, right?"

"So how does all that help us in the end?"

"I'm not sure, but we'll have a base from which to work. We can decide on what to do then, but let's find out what the hell we're dealing with first!"

"So, how do you propose to get all that information if you don't trust the contractor's records?"

"Go back into the school!"

Carter looked at Sable, then at Mathis, shocked.

"Go back into the school? Mathis, you're crazy! We just barely got out of there the first time, and you wanna go back?"

"I didn't say *we*, did I? I know a couple of people who would be willing to go with me, for a price."

"How much?"

"I dunno! Few hundred bucks, I guess, maybe more, maybe less."

"I can handle *that*," Carter offered.

"Good," said Mathis, relieved. "I'll get on the stick immediately. Know exactly what I have to do."

"And me?" Carter asked curiously.

"Someone's got to go down to the Hall of Records," said Mathis.

"Yeah, well, I can do that, but I ain't about to go back into the basement. How you gonna keep from getting caught?"

"Remember the videotape machine that scans the place every hour?"

"Yeah."

"We'll just replace the reel with a blank before we leave, that's all!"

"How do you know it's just a closed-circuit setup? I mean, suppose it's being monitored somewhere?"

"Don't know that it's not, but I got a connection with someone who can tell me when he sees the setup."

"Who are these people you know? They gonna keep their mouths shut?"

"Really will! Brothers I knew in Nam. Got a whole lot of training but couldn't get no jobs when they got out. You know the story," he said in an obvious self-reference. "One works as a security guard at some honky company in Studio City. Nigger knows more about electronics than most engineers. The other dude hustles like me, somewhere in Chicago. I'll have to track him down, but I know who to talk to. Motherfucker knows construction like the back of your hand. He was in explosives—you know, demolition. Army sent him to school for a year—not to learn about blowing up shit, but to learn about the stuff he had to blow up. Very heavy brother!"

"Mathis, what are we going to do once we get all this information? Will you please answer me *that*!" Carter asked in desperation.

"Shit, Doc, let's worry about that when the time comes, OK?" Carter nodded his head and continued to file his nails, long since shaped by the emory board.

"Give me that! You gonna wear it out before it's over!" Sable said, snatching the emory board and placing it in her purse beside her.

Carter stood up and stretched his tired limbs. It had been quite a night, and morning would soon be upon them. Tomorrow he would call in sick and spend the balance of the day downtown. He would have to get some rest if he was to function at all.

Mathis left at five as Carter and Sable retired. The morning would bring a new day and with it some answers.

CHAPTER 11

THE SHABBILY DRESSED white woman behind the counter was of no help to Carter. She had only been on the job five weeks and knew little more than her name. The Hall of Records was a classic example of bureaucratic mind-boggling. Employees of the system had to constantly consult supervisors before anyone could make a decision. The machinery was paralyzed with apathy and ineptitude. Rules and regulations had to be reviewed because no one had ever read them in the first place.

Finally, after what seemed like hours of wrangling with minor departmental officials, a secretary, very seductive and very white, approached Carter to advise him that he could secure a release from the district administrator in the Bureau of Public Documents on the second floor. Once the release was signed, she was sure that there would be no further problems with the availability of the documents sought.

She was right. The administrator was quite proper, obviously bright, and decidedly homosexual.

"Dr. Carter?" he asked in a honey-coated tone, flashing his polished fingernails about the papers on the desk.

"Yes. You're Mr. Andrews?"

"Ahhh yes, that's right, that's right. I do hope you weren't terribly, terribly put out by the girls upstairs, but they do have their regulations, you know." The width of his green tie and the high-combed pompadour hair style gave him a comical appearance. His yellow pin-striped shirt was matched only by the color of his dentures, and the aftershave cologne he wore did little to cut through the stench of his foul-smelling breath that hung in the air after every word spoken. He wore a blue suit that still had the price tag attached to the buttons on the cuffs of the sleeves.

He motioned for Carter to be seated and picked up the phone.

"Marva, sweetheart, does it really take you that long to bring the papers in here?" He never took his eyes off Carter throughout the conversation, smiling continuously as if anything less might detract from his appeal. The secretary arrived. Her short dress and thin legs made her look like an ostrich as she bent over the desk to clarify a point with the administrator.

"Would you sign here, please?" he asked, the frozen smile melting from muscle fatigue. Carter moved to the desk, pen in hand, and began writing his name next to the check mark in red ink. As he did so, the administrator put his hand on top of Carter's, slowly stroking his fingers.

134

"Do you like the way my hands feel?" Carter asked without moving or looking his way.

Thinking that it was an acceptance, the administrator answered eagerly, "Oh, yes, yes I do!"

"That's good, because I'm going to amputate yours and shove them down your throat. That way you can feel your ass, too!" Carter turned his head slowly toward the administrator, who quickly withdrew his arm and sat down in his chair, pretending to busy himself with the papers on the desk. He said nothing more.

Carter walked across the hall to the records room and handed the slip to the girl behind the counter. In three minutes she returned arms full of tubes, papers, and folders. She placed them on the counter top and directed Carter to the reading room next door. He moved the pile to the next room and settled himself in the chair facing the desk.

It would be quite a task.

At four-forty-five the young woman announced that it was closing time and he would have to return tomorrow if he wished to continue with his review. He declined, having written down all the essential facts on notebook paper. He thanked her for her cooperation and departed even more depressed than he was when he came. It had been a trying day, and the information obtained did little in the way of relieving his anxiety. It would disturb a lot of people at the meeting that Mathis had called tonight.

The first to voice his disturbance was Mathis.

"What do you mean there's no architectural plans for the basement? There has to be! Nigger can't build a goddamn school without a sound structural foundation!" Carter had found the plans, but they did not include any design features for a basement. Even the rooms that were a normal part of the school were either missing or nonexistent.

"Who was the architect?" snapped Mathis, pacing the floor like a toy soldier.

"Carson-Porter, Inc. They also built it."

"You mean they were the *contractors,* too?"

"Yeah, that's right."

"Oh, then it's easy. We just check it out with them. No problem!"

"One slight problem," said Carter, his voice betraying still another mystery.

"I'm waiting," said Mathis, blowing short puffs of smoke impatiently from his mouth, the ashes dangling precipitously from the end of the cigarette.

"Well, it seems that the American Architectural Society, the Los Angeles Architectural Cooperative, and the National Association of Architectural Contractors have no such listing for a firm by that name. I ran a check on them this afternoon. They don't *exist!*"

"What the fuck you talking about, man? If they bid on the project, they got to exist!"

"They bid on it all right—I read the offer. I also checked out the address given at the time: a parking lot next door to Lincoln Savings downtown! Been there for ten years! School was built in 68—rather, it was completed in 68—was started in mid-67."

Mathis rubbed the back of his head pensively, puffing on his cigarette, the smoke drifting across the room like clouds in the sky. "Two years after the riots," he said softly.

"What?" said Sable, still hoarse from the previous night.

"I was thinking out loud. I said it was built two years after the riots."

She acknowledged the clarification but remained silent. Carter continued.

"I also checked on the payroll vouchers and the subcontractors. Very interesting, I *must* say! There were no independent subcontractors. They were all owned by or subsidiaries of Carson-Porter, Inc. Oh, yes! I checked with the corporate commissioner: he never heard of Carson-Porter either!"

"Bingo!" Mathis said. "Do not pass, go straight to jail. *Ain't* this a bitch! Motherfucking honkies do anything they want and then got nerve for wanting to put a nigger in jail for stealing a loaf of bread!"

"Wait! I haven't *finished* yet. The payroll vouchers were all cashed through B of A, a legitimate account but closed immediately after completion of the project. Signatures on the checks and the signature cards matched, but the social security number is nonexistent."

"Isn't that beautiful?" said Sable, smiling cynically. "The perfect cover right down to the social security number! That is *deep,* baby!"

"Yeah, you right on that, baby," said Carter. "Ain't no way to trace the man when he wants to stay hid." He smiled and relaxed in the chair.

"Yes there is," Mathis blurted out, extinguishing the cigarette in the ceramic ash tray on the coffee table.

"Oh tell us, *please* tell us!" said Sable, laughing cynically through her hoarseness.

"No—seriously. There is. That's why I want my boys to go back into the school yard and go through it with a fine tooth comb. All that equipment in there? Someone had to make it, right? So if someone had to make it, then it's just a matter of going to that person and finding out who bought it. *Simple!*" Mathis had been able to locate one of the men he had mentioned earlier, the electrician, but the most crucial one was out of town and it would take a while yet to locate him. He felt that he would have a handle on him by midweek.

Several days went by before Mathis called for another meeting of the principals at Mafundi. The weather had changed again, and the Santa Ana winds bathed the city in hot, dry breezes that kept the streets full and the housing projects empty. Theaters were packed with folks who wanted to believe that Shaft was real, watching superstuds and superniggers in living techniblack playing roles created by biased fantasies of white writers who never went to Harlem and thought Watts was a power company. Short-sleeved shirts, platform shoes, wide-brimmed hats, and the bimonthly check from the Department of Public Social Services kept everyone complacent.

There was a conference on drug abuse held at the Beverly Hills Hotel, a task force meeting on the problems of rape held at UCLA, and a two-point-seven million-dollar grant for the study of sickle cell anemia was awarded to a major white institution that had never previously even considered studying the disease until the government announced that it would subsidize any effort. The community rocked back and forth in its cradle of inertia, confident that freedom was just around the corner. Belafonte was appearing at the Greek, and Sly Stone had just released his new album. Muhammad Ali won his fight, and Richard Nixon lost his. Black gangs continued to annihilate each other using guns, pungi sticks, and profanities as they desperately sought to define their roles and establish limits for a responsibility their parents had long since abdicated, their preoccupation on survival and the treacherous seduction of racist liberalism.

Robin Niles was cool.

At thirty he had mastered everything it took to get ahead, but somehow he couldn't get a job. He was quiet, reserved, and witty when necessary. He was easy to get along with and aloof when suspicious. His brain was analytical and well trained. Carter could see why Mathis wanted him on the team. His bushy natural and full beard framed his black face, and under a halo he would have looked like a saint. Short and stocky, he walked like a football player in full uniform, slow, awkward, and slue-footed. It would be a mistake to judge him by his appearance. If he had to kill you, he would—without hesitation. If he had to kill anybody on this operation, it wouldn't be the first time. His background in demolition and construction made him necessary, but the fact that he could be trusted made him invaluable.

Donald Falcon resembled a man just coming off a drunk. His hair was seldom combed, and his clothes looked tacky. The Pinkerton uniform he wore helped to hide his appearance, but his manner and personality had little to recommend them. He was crude and gross. From the South, his speech made him sound retarded, his brogue as heavy as his frame. He was obviously overweight and, Carter guessed, also hypertensive. Despite his less than inspiring appearance, he was prompt and attentive.

Mathis now had his team. The only unresolved issue was money. The purpose of the meeting at Mafundi was to settle that issue and lay the groundwork for the second entry. The two men listened intently as Mathis and Carter unfolded what must have sounded

138

like a story from the pen of Ian Fleming. When they were finished, the two newcomers looked at each other in silent amazement, disbelief still in the air.

"You really saw a jail, a real jail?" Niles asked, stroking his beard repeatedly, his steel-gray eyes fixed on the man in front of him.

"I think concentration camp is a more appropriate choice of words," said Carter, trying to avoid Niles's gaze.

"Concentration camp? How many people will it hold?" Falcon asked.

"Five hundred at the most," Mathis said flatly.

"Kinda small for a concentration camp, ain't it? I mean, it would have to be a lot bigger than *that* if they were planning to get rid of all twenty-five million of us!"

"That's why we need you," Mathis replied. "You've gotta find out what their plans are for it!"

Niles pursed his lips, looked at the ceiling, and continued to stroke his beard. There was a brief pause before he spoke.

"I see. You want us to go down to the jail or camp or whatever, and bring back information, right?"

Mathis nodded his head in agreement.

"Any chance of getting caught?"

"Yes!" Carter exclaimed. "There is a complete closed-circuit television set up with videotape, like Mathis said. Don't know if it's picked up on a distant monitor, though. And there might be other alarm systems we don't know about." As he spoke, he turned to look at Falcon who sat cross-legged on the floor in front of the file cabinet.

"Whatchu gonna do wid all this information we bring you?" Falcon asked benignly, his slow drawl amusing to those listening.

"Haven't decided yet."

"Gonna cost you some money!" said Falcon matter-of-factly.

"Really is," sighed Niles, his attention once again on the men in front of him.

Mathis looked at Carter to indicate responsibility. They in turn also looked at Carter, waiting. He picked it up from there.

"It's open. What do you think it's worth?"

Niles continued to stroke his beard, looking first at Mathis and then at Carter and back to Mathis again. "Couple o' grand at least, plus any legal expenses if I get caught." Mathis winced. He had told Carter two hundred give or take a hundred, but two thousand he *never* expected!

Before either man could answer, Niles spoke up again: "Ain't child's play you asking. Already got two dudes killed!"

Carter looked at Falcon, still lost in thought. "And you?"

"Same," he said. "And that's cheap, considerin'."

"I hear you. Right on, brother!" said Niles, holding his flat palm extended.

They waited in silence for Carter to respond. He did, without prompting or coercion. "OK, four grand plus contigencies. I can handle it."

Mathis breathed a sigh of relief and walked to the drinking fountain adjacent to the file cabinet. The soothing chill of refrigerated water trickled down his throat, a welcome companion in the heat of the day. Carter pulled out his checkbook, but Niles waved him off.

"It's all right, Doc. I trust you. I know Mathis too well to think he'd be involved with anyone unreliable. I'll get mine when I come out. If I don't," he smiled, "send it to my old lady. She'll need it." He laughed loudly and returned to stroking his beard.

"Well, you can gimme mine now, Doc," said Falcon sheepishly, stretching his cramped legs in front of him. Carter obliged, handing him the check.

"Well," said Niles, jumping to his feet, "now that it's settled, let's get it on, hey!" He popped his finger, snapped his head back, closed his eyes, and began singing the song made popular by Marvin Gaye, clapping his hands in rhythm.

Mathis broke open the diagrams of the school, and they spent the balance of the hot Saturday afternoon reviewing and planning for another entry. It would take place in seven days, on a Sunday night as had the last one. They would have to gamble on the weather forecast clear through the end of the month.

The week passed uneventfully. The hot, stagnant air from the Santa Anas moved lazily through the basin en route to the northern part of the state. The smoggy sediment burned the eyes and ate away at the lungs of children already racked by malnutrition and marginal health care. Black elected officials made bland speeches attacking the food stamp program while supporting the efforts of the newly funded Center for the Study of Violence to be located in Westwood. Its clientele, primarily black, would be drawn from Watts for experimentation in behavior control through brain-probe procedures.

Niles stayed with Mathis, who was single, in his apartment in the Jungle. It was a comfortably furnished two-bedroom bachelor apartment with wall-to-wall carpeting and indirect lighting. Because of the tremendously high crime rate, each window and door was secured by burglar bars, which spoiled the courtyard view of the once tropical-appearing apartment complex.

Since Mathis lived in the street he was seldom there, leaving Niles to himself. The Jungle provided Niles with a great deal of feminine entertainment, its high ratio of single and divorced women living alone creating a buyer's market. Sable had wanted to introduce him to one of her friends, but when she found out he was married she backed off. She did, however, invite him to dinner each evening along with Falcon, who usually refused, only accepting the offer when he was unable to line up female companionship for the evening. Sable saw him as a very intense person despite his reserve, and his ideas and philosophies paralleled hers with one exception— he was a male chauvinist pig from his heart!

They carried the project off without a hitch, Mathis switching the existing videotape with a blank just prior to leaving. They spent two hours in the jail facility itself and returned with several pages of notes. The results were interesting, revealing, and, as expected, did little to minimize anyone's anxiety about the whole thing. The critique was at Carter's the next morning. They had breakfast and adjourned to the den, now lit by the bright morning sun as it made the slow trek to the other side of the earth. Niles was the first to speak: "Well are you ready for Pandora's box?"

"Right on!"

"Yeah, well let me run it down to you." He leafed through a pile of papers on the table, checking the page numbers to make certain they were in order. Satisfied, he began.

"Let me give you this information first. Then you ask questions later if you want. Most of this is technical and will require explanation, so I'll try and give you stuff you can understand, OK?" Each nodded his agreement.

"To begin with, the cement is standard, made from powdered lime and clay in a ratio . . . I'd say . . . of two to three; commercially produced, can't be traced. The concrete that is the final product that the jail is made from is in a mixture of one, three, five to ten. To explain further: one part gravel, three parts cement, and five parts sand in a ratio of ten parts of water. Rest assured it's very solid! Whoever contracted the job definitely knew his shit, no doubt about it! Now, the actual construction time—oh, by the way, people, you missed an additional floor. There is another sub-basement, where most of the electrical equipment is located, but it only has one corridor."

"How could they have built it without anyone detecting it?" asked Sable. "I mean, there was no scaffolding or panels; it was only a two-story school. Someone was bound to have been watching the construction!"

"Right you are, sister, but they used lift-slabbing—that's why!"

"What the hell is lift-slabbing?" Carter asked, annoyed at his own ignorance.

"OK, let me explain it so everyone understands." Mathis smiled wryly. They would get their four grand's worth and *then* some!

"They poured the foundation for the subbasement—after the plumbing had been installed for the school of course—then they poured the roof of the subbasement, which would be the floor of the prison—got it?" he asked, his eyes viewing the bewilderment in the room.

"You mean they put one floor on top of another floor?" Carter asked.

"Well, yes, basically that's right, only they weren't connected.

142

Once the roof or the floor, if you want to call it that, is set they then build another floor on top of that one, which was to serve as the roof of the prison but also the floor of the school! Everyone follow me so far?" He asked that, knowing they were totally lost.

"They built three floors, one on top of another? Is that what you're saying?"

"Right on, baby. Then they placed hydraulic jacks on top of the subbasement slab but under the prison floor, and slowly jacked up two slabs, the school floor and the prison floor. When it reached basement level, they installed their pilings and support structures, removing the jacks, and placed them under the school floor but on top of the now-elevated prison floor and repeated the same thing.

"When they reached ground level, they placed all of their supporting members—which were well built, by the way—and removed the jacks and, *presto,* two floors in existence before work ever commenced on the school itself. It's obvious to me that it deceived everyone, even the school officials." Niles drew a small diagram to clarify his point, which it did, to everyone's relief.

"So what really happened . . ." Mathis was cut off abruptly by an impatient Niles.

"What happened was they built the basement *first,* which then allowed them to install the prison facility undetected while they were building the classrooms at the same time. No one would suspect or question the bringing in of materials during the construction period! Obviously, they had to time it just right—that is, the school had to be finished at the same time the prison was finished."

"Kiss my ass, can you believe *that!*" Carter was amazed. "Where did you get all that information? I mean, just from that one trip down there you could tell that much?"

"There's more. That particular technique, while we're on the subject, is used almost exclusively in the construction of skyscrapers. No one would ever lift-slab a two-story building; it would be too much. Somebody had big bucks!"

"No shit! More like Uncle, huh?" Sable was applauded by the group in unison.

"Let's see." He leafed through more papers and organized several in front of him. "Plumbing was nothing but the best, used . . ." He stopped in midsentence, recalling a thought before continuing. "To digress a moment, the steel used was high quality. I've never seen quality construction like this except on federal projects. No two-story school in anybody's ghetto has construction like this one. . . . Where was I?"

"Plumbing," said Carter, his attention unbroken.

"Right. Used nothing but the best. All copper tubing throughout. They tapped the main plumbing system and used the conventional water route for waste disposal. Very smoothly done! Has boost pumps to keep pressure elevated at the school level so as not to arouse attention. Uses butane gas so as to avoid attention by the gas company."

"How do they keep from being picked up by DWP?" asked Sable, striking a provocative pose unintentionally, her breasts bulging through the green jersey sweater as she leaned forward on the couch. ˜

"As many faucets and light fixtures as the school has, plus all those bathrooms, it would go unnoticed.

"Let me say another word about the steel. Supergrade! Well tempered! Usually there are identifying marks that reveal the foundry, but in this case none of the steel had marks. I'm speaking about the steel used to make the cell bars and what-have-you. Can't say about the reinforcement steel in the concrete. Obviously, someone either etched the markings off, or they were ordered that way! But at any rate tensile strength is high, chrome moley grade, all nitrided, that is, hardened and without flaws. I magnafluxed a random sample to see if there were any cracks—didn't find a thing!"

"What is a magnaflux?" asked Mathis, as fascinated as the rest.

"Would take a long time to explain it, but it's basically a material you put on metal that shows up minute cracks and flaws not normally visible to the naked eye. Presence of cracks and flaws usually means fatigue and stress have weakened the metal so that it isn't structurally sound, OK?" Mathis indicated comprehension, and Niles continued with his class.

"All bathroom and kitchen fixtures, like porcelain bowls, sinks, and towel racks, were unmarked. No way they can be traced to

144

original sources. All glasses, silverware, cooking utensils, eating facilities, even the garbage disposals are unmarked. And, Doc, of particular interest to you, I went through the dispensary. Did you know they had a small X-ray unit, lead walls and the like? The X-ray unit was not marked, but I recognized the unit as being a Ritter—saw a lot of them in Nam. But dig this! They got a small operating room, nothing fancy, but well equipped. All the surgical instruments, and I would have expected to see Bard Parker, were blanks—no identification whatsoever! Even the syringes were not identified. All fluids were marked with tape, but the original labels had been removed. There was something really strange, too. I would have never expected to find it in an operating room! I mean a cardiogram machine was there, but there was also a machine that looked similar except the tracing tape . . . that what you call it?"

"Yes."

"Well, the tracing tape was much wider."

"Wider? Did it have any other marks or numbers on it?"

"No! What kind of machine would it be?"

Carter knew what kind of machine it was. He looked at Sable for a moment and then at the group before he answered, and in doing so, laughed cynically as he spoke, his head shaking from side to side.

"It's an electroencephalograph for reading brain waves of people."

"Why would it be in a dispensary like that, Doc?" asked Mathis, sensing Carter's discomfort.

"You're right! It's not normally part of an emergency room or an operating room. I suspect such a facility would be used for psychosurgery—behavior modification by brain-surgery techniques!"

"Ain't that a bitch! You sure, Doc?" said Niles, stroking his beard.

"That would be my guess!"

"Damn, all them niggers in the jail gonna get their brains picked out!" said Falcon, his eyes wide in fascination. "The man really has it in for us, huh?"

"Now I understand," said Sable despondently. "Don't need

more than 500 cells. They could run the brothers through that place in shifts and wouldn't none of us know about it till it was our turn!"

"Yeah," said Mathis angrily. "Be just like it was with the Jews. They refused to believe Hitler was exterminating them right up to the day the trucks backed up to their doors!"

Carter sat lost in thought. Never in his life did he ever anticipate being involved in anything so horrendous. He asked if Niles was through, the group fatigued, despite its avid attention. Niles held up two fingers and related briefly some minor things about the construction. Finished, he asked for questions, but he had answered most of them earlier. Sable suggested a break for coffee before hearing Falcon, a good move since he would prove to be no more reassuring than Niles.

Thirty minutes of coffee and the Jazz Crusaders relaxed them. The sun was angling through the glass doors, its rays moving slowly toward the wall. Carter abruptly stopped the record album, and they assembled again.

Falcon surprised them. As he began to speak, his speech pattern changed and his words became more distinct. He had either rehearsed what he was going to say, or he became so involved in his work that he experienced a different part of himself, seldom seen. Carter guessed it was the latter. Like Niles, he had taken extensive notes on what he had seen, but found it necessary to draw numerous diagrams in advance to explain what he anticipated would be difficult for them to visualize. This proved to be very helpful.

"Where should I start, folks? This is some complicated shit we dealin' with. If you think the man got his shit together from the construction end, wait until you see what he done with the electronics!"

"Stop all that bullshitting, Falcon, and get on with it," said Mathis.

"Right! OK, first of all, everyone here in this room is lucky that they not in *jail,* and the only reason you *ain't* is because the school alarm didn't go off! That door we all went through from the playground? Well, it's so far from the molding that it didn't trip the alarm, which, I might add, is one of the best that's made. Very sophisticated. The school alarm obviously goes directly to the police station. I can't understand why they didn't fix it after those kids broke in!"

"What about the prison? Is *it* equipped with an alarm?" asked Carter.

"Believe it or not, no! Not the kind we're talking about. The setup there is the television camera and videotape. Near as I can determine, it's strictly a closed-circuit job. Obviously the dudes check the tape every sixty or so hours because it's set to scan for one minute every hour and it's only a one-hour tape. If you wanta find out who it is, just wait there for sixty hours and you'll see!"

"Anything unusual about the camera or monitors?"

"Naw. All the identifications have been removed, but it's a Sony, no doubt about that! Could have been bought anywhere."

"How do the lights work?" asked Mathis curiously.

"Not complicated, all connected to the main switch, which is tied in by relay to the timer. The whole place uses circuit breakers; no fuses!"

"Hey, that's great. All we have to do is check with the Edison folks to see who uses all that electricity," said Mathis, jumping to his feet in triumph.

"Don't you wish you could!" laughed Falcon loudly. "First of all, every bit of electrical equipment is supplied by diesel-driven generators, 60,000 watts. These are direct water-cooling units with a back-up power supply from 360-horsepower Perkins diesels—two of them at that! There's a 10,000-gallon tank beneath the subbasement that Niles mentioned earlier.

"Got enough fuel to run the jail for several months at a time. I can't prove it, but I'm pretty sure it's filled from an adjacent manhole located in the street intersection. But that ain't all! As a reserve in case all else fails, they got four—no, five gasoline-powered 4-cylinder engines that are lightweight and small. My guess would be they rate about 30 horsepower each. The tachometers all read 3500 rpm's. More than likely they got oversized water jackets throughout, with three-sixteenth's section castings. Each one has a 12-volt ignition, a 12-volt, 35-amp alternator, automatic temperature-control thermostat, a rubber impeller-type water pump, a mechanical fuel pump, and, last but not least, a separate hand sump pump for changing oil."

"So what does all that mean, man? And damn it, tell us in *English*—shit!" said Mathis, somewhat irritated.

Falcon shook his head, mumbling to himself. Trying to explain technical material to laymen was a bitch!

"It means that if all external power sources were eliminated for some particular reason, the prison could function for months, maybe years before needing any additional power." He observed the somewhat confused look of the members in the room, but kept talking.

"Now let's talk about communication; very heavy indeed! First of all, they got two systems of communication, see, a self-contained radio-telephone-type setup, and a more conventional external-connected telephone system. The self-contained system is a transistorized solid-state radio-telephone, a marine type actually, now that I think about it. Anyway, it has about two or three hundred watts' output, front-panel priority button for instant monitoring, and a dual-conversion superhet receiver that probably has minimal sensitivity, low battery drain from a 12-volt power source, and a voice-modulated high-gain mike. Now they also have . . ."

"Wait a minute, wait a minute! Man, don't none of us know what the fuck you're *talking* about! What does all that jive mean in *English*? In *English*! Understand?" Mathis was visibly annoyed now.

"Amen!" said Sable. Her facial expression mirrored her innermost thoughts: total lack of comprehension!

"Look, people, this is what the man has in the basement! I don't know if I can explain it any simpler. Just gonna have to bear with me. I'll break it down as best I can, OK?"

"Yeah, yeah, man, go on!" said Mathis. Completely exasperated, he sank deep into the bean-bag chair and detached himself from the group. Niles lit a cigarette but continued to sit quietly, stroking his beard. Carter, seated next to Sable, took advantage of everyone's attention focused on Falcon and ran his hand up between her legs. She recoiled, clamped her knees together, and removed his hand without looking his way. Falcon began again.

"Like I said before I was so rudely interrupted, they have a more conventional telephone system that can be hooked up to the Bell system when operative. They have ten 584C panels, each with twenty-four dozen 400 KTU units to feed the relay systems. They tapped the lines of the school but have kept the connection open, obviously to avoid suspicion on the part of the phone company."

"Hey, my man," said Niles, enveloped in smoke, "what does it all mean? *That's* what the man is paying you for!"

"Right. Well actually, to make a long story short, they have two forms of communication, a shortwave setup and a regular telephone setup that can be plugged into the outside system. All lighting is by 110 AC, just like in this house, but there is a redundant wiring system to the convertor that allows them to switch to a 12-volt system in case of an emergency. Baby, the only thing that jail ain't got is food. Otherwise, it is completely self-sufficient!"

They remained silent for a moment as Falcon reshuffled his papers and placed them back in the attaché case. Despite his inability to conform to middle-class expectations in explaining things, they knew his material was accurate even if they didn't understand it. They also knew that they had discovered something that could get them all killed if they were identified in any way.

It was noon, and the room had grown dimmer as the sun slipped toward the west. Looking through the glass doors, Carter observed the heat waves rising from the concrete as the water in the pool settled motionless in its porcelain basin on this hot, windless afternoon. Sable suggested a swim to relax them, but it fell on deaf ears. Even Niles, who had initially seen himself as performing a job and getting out, now seemed preoccupied.

They had a quickly prepared lunch at Sizzler's on Santa Barbara and returned to the house for further discussion that yielded relatively little until Falcon, in his ignorant-sounding way, mentioned something that bothered everyone.

"Anybody here ever think that they might have jails in other cities?" he asked casually.

"In other *cities?* What makes you think that?" asked Mathis.

"Shit, the man built a concentration camp under a ghetto school for only one reason: to exterminate niggers like Hitler killed the Jews. So he has to have more than one, 'cause they's more than one ghetto, right?"

Mathis looked at Niles pensively, then at Carter, who was busy trying to convince himself that Falcon's remark had no basis. Sable picked up the ball and ran: "You mean there might be one in every city that has a ghetto?"

"I wouldn't say every city," said Niles stroking his beard as he looked about the room, "but I think it's reasonable to assume that every city with any sizable black population bears looking at. That means Chicago, New York, Philadelphia, Newark, Saint Louis, Washington, D.C., Atlanta for sure, and maybe New Orleans."

"Damn," Sable said. "A whole network of underground concentration camps all over the country! Do you know what that means? Shit, all niggers have to do is just push the man a little too far and it's all over for us—pow!" she shouted, thrusting her clenched fist straight ahead.

"I got news for you, baby," said Mathis, his face frozen with a cynical smile. "It's already over for niggers. Whitey already had it planned from the very beginning. He just gonna keep us here as long as he feels it's to his benefit. It's obvious that our usefulness to him has begun to diminish. Why do you think he built that jail? He plans to go into action very soon, and . . ."

"Wait a minute, Mathis," said Carter, sensing the uneasiness settling over the room. "Let's not get paranoid about this thing. I mean, we don't have any proof that there are others. No sense going hog wild."

Sable felt the goose bumps form on her skin. "How do we know there aren't, huh? Shit, baby, looking at a concentration camp under a school in Watts is reason enough to be paranoid as hell. Damn, it ain't there just for folks to look at!"

"So what do you suggest? Check every city in the country? People would lock all of us up as *insane* if you went around telling about this. Not *me!*"

"Would you finance someone who would?" Niles said, his hand

motionless on his beard as he waited for Carter's answer. All eyes were focused on Niles, whose comment was obviously serious.

"You mean pay people like I did you and Falcon?" Niles shook his head in the affirmative.

"Aw, man, I don't have that kind of bread but . . ." He turned and gazed toward the pool, the afternoon shadows now slowly approaching to cool the unsheltered yard. Sable fidgeted on the couch, the grating of her pantyhose annoying as she repeatedly crossed and uncrossed her legs. Carter returned Niles's stare and shifted his eyes to the wall behind him. He stiffened in his position and in a softer, uncertain tone, finished his sentence: "I think I might know someone who would!"

"Who?" said Sable, surprised as her head snapped around toward him.

"Walker," he said blandly. "How much are we talking about— ten, maybe twenty grand?"

"Well, let's see, we're talking about air fare for at least five people plus hotel expenses, food, transportation, and . . ." He paused to catch his breath, sighed as if hesitant to continue, but did so reluctantly after coercion from Carter.

"And what?"

"Well, it's going to be a full-time job. Someone has to pay for lost wages or some kind of compensation for their time, plus any legal expenses if they get caught, providing, of course, that ain't no one killed in the process! Might only take a few weeks, maybe a couple of months if they do a thorough search of each ghetto. But yeah, I'd say it might cost ten to twenty grand for the right people. You got to get people you can trust and who know the city, and that means recruiting in every ghetto."

"Why new people in each city? Why can't the same people check each place out? Hell, Niles, that's just added expense!" said Carter, his eye fixed on Niles's hair-enshrouded face.

"Right on, Doc. But, don't never go into another community without first getting someone from that community involved. Quickest way I know to get yourself killed! Look at it this way: Whitey thinks of ghettos as foreign countries, and since he thinks that way,

151

he feels that all he has to do is just walk in and do his shit. It used to be like that till niggers woke up to what was happening. Now, if whitey wants to do his shit, he just buys a nigger from that particular ghetto and lets him be the front man.

"Understand now? All we have to do is the same thing, except we ain't out to rip the brothers off! We're out to try and find out whether or not whitey has built any more of these goddamn extermination camps, or whatever they are!"

"Why not just tell the ghettos themselves and let them look on their own? Man, them community agencies would love a project like this."

"Falcon," said Niles, shaking his head in resignation, "are you crazy? Do you have any idea of what would happen if niggers all over the country even suspected that the man had carried out something like this?"

"No. What?" said Falcon indignantly, resenting the remark.

"Hey, baby, niggers would panic and tear this country *up* and, in so doing, would be systematically annihilated."

"*So*, maybe that's better than the way we living now!" Falcon countered.

"Man, the brothers deserve more than that—shit! Hell, we built this country. You gonna let him have it just 'cause he don't like niggers? No way! Look, a dead nigger ain't no good to no one, 'cept three people: the preacher, 'cause he can make his reputation on the eulogy; the mortician, 'cause he can make his money when he's buried; and whitey, 'cause to him the only good nigger is a dead nigger! Ain't no reason for us to give him the excuse he needs to kill us without exercising his conscience. No indeed!"

"He's got a point, Falcon," said Carter, sensing the tension developing between the two. "I think it's best we keep it to ourselves until we find out whether or not there *are* any more camps. No sense in creating a panic. By the time the media gets through with it there'd be nothing but chaos. Let's cool it for now." Carter scanned the room for agreement. It was unanimous.

"Looks like you found a hornets' nest," said Falcon.

Niles laughed and stamped his feet several times on the rug.

"Yeah, at least one of them, brother," he said, holding out his hand for Falcon to slap. He did, and the atmosphere was once again relaxed. Carter put the latest album by Herbie Mann on the turntable, and they listened in silence as the sounds of the muted flute filled their ears.

Later that evening, after they had eaten dinner at Charlie Brown's in the Marina, Carter brought the conversation back to his afternoon point.

"So you think it best to hire people in each city to avoid any static?"

"Yeah," said Niles, "but it wouldn't require a whole lot of dudes, just two or three at the most. Look, there are a lot of consistencies that narrow the search down for us."

"How so?"

"Well, for one, we know this one was built right after the riots in '65, right? So there's no reason to think that the same pattern didn't follow in Detroit, Chicago, and everywhere else we mentioned."

"But . . ."

"Wait, hear me out, OK? Now another point to consider is the fact that it has to be fairly new construction. I mean, there's no way they gonna build something of that magnitude without starting from the ground up, so all we have to do is find where any construction took place after '65 and '66. After all, they ain't that much new stuff in the ghetto, 'cause unless it's city, county, or government funded, the banks won't touch it! I think our best bet is to check out all the new schools, churches, apartment houses—things like that. Shouldn't be too hard, 'cause there ain't no money coming into the ghettos. People avoid that like the plague, man!"

"I'm hip," said Sable. "Until it's time to build some commercial freeway, then they take nigger's property and give 'em damn near nothin' for it—shit!"

"Anyway, Doc, you said you knew someone who might front the money for this kind of thing."

"Yeah, Leviah Walker. He's a colleague; big-time money man and all that. But he keeps his mouth shut. He might be willing to do it, especially since it's for the community. He digs shit like that."

"Then call him, shit, right now," said Falcon, "and let's get it on!"

Carter made several unsuccessful attempts to locate Walker through his inefficient exchange.

Sable had the answer. "Now gentlemen, you know it's late." Her head nodded in the direction of the glass door where they could see daylight fading to darkness. "Where do you think most male chauvinistic pigs go at night? My suggestion—is if you want to reach someone who doesn't particularly want to be found at this moment—would be to contact the woman he's sleeping with, and that's Vashti!" She smiled sheepishly at the group and waited for the phone to answer.

She was a prophet!

A brief conversation with Walker on the phone brought him to the house in an hour, his playmate hooked to his arm.

He listened quietly as the story unfolded. When they had finished, he asked a number of questions to clarify points of confusion and then asked the question nobody wanted to hear.

"What do you plan to do if you find any others? And if not, what do you plan to do about the one here?"

Each looked at the other furtively, not knowing how to respond. Niles took the initiative.

"Well, Doc, we had sort of planned to wait and see if we found any more before we decided what to do."

"Is one any less terrible than ten?" he asked searchingly.

"No, I guess not," answered Niles.

"Well then, what are you going to do about the one you found? I mean it doesn't really make any difference how many you find if you don't know what you're going to do when you find them! Whatever you decided to do about this one here, you should do the same about the others, if there are any others."

They looked at each other again, puzzled. Walker, irritated at their indecisiveness, admonished them.

"You know, the one thing that kills most black folks is their inability to make a decision about anything!"

"Well, we sure as hell ain't going to turn it into a museum for niggers to look at!" said Mathis angrily.

"Don't get bent out of shape! I'm not attacking anyone personally. It's just that I've seen it happen so many times, over and over again, that it makes me sick! I agree with you that you can't afford to let the communities know about this—it's too explosive!"

"Then who do we tell, Walker?" asked Carter.

"Nobody, *that's* who!"

"Shit, if you ain't gonna tell nobody, then what's the point of even bothering to see if there *are* any others?"

"Now you see what I mean!" said Walker, setting the group up for the kill. Niles moved within rifle range.

"What do *you* suggest we do?"

"Destroy them!"

"Destroy them! You mean blow them up? Just like that? I mean, no public charge or announcement—nothing?" Mathis's face was contorted in bewilderment.

"That's what I would do. Fix it so they could never be used!"

"Suppose we don't find any more? Just this one here in Watts?" asked Sable curiously, her light eyes dancing from face to face.

"Same," said Walker. "Blow it off the face of the earth!"

He knew what was bugging them. If they did as he suggested, there would be no public accolade, no recognition, no grandstanding! He ran it down to them, and when he finished, they understood. It was obviously the only thing they could do. Black folks need never know the concentration camps ever existed!

"Look," he continued, "you want me to finance an expedition back east that might just be a wild-goose chase. Now I'm not willing to spend money for that alone, but I am willing to spend money if it means that any prison you find gets eliminated!"

"That'll cost you some more bread!" said Niles, masturbating his beard.

"Let's assume we find five, OK? Do you know how hard it is to get the kind of explosives that it'll take to demolish just *one* of these? That thing is a damn fortress, man, and any kind of explosion severe enough to damage or destroy it will also bring down whatever is on top of it—in this case, the school!"

"Forget about the cost! Can it be done? I mean, can the material be gotten? The hell with the structure on top. That's secondary at this point."

"Oh yeah, the stuff can be bought all right, but it means paying off a lot of people with a lot of money. Gonna need some lead time, too, 'cause we don't know how many more jails we'll find, if any!"

"Assume that you find six. How much would it cost?" said Walker, pulling out his name-engraved Parker ballpoint.

"If there were six—oh, I'd say maybe fifty, sixty thousand bills, and that's everything. Course the longer we search, you might have to add a few dollars for transportation and lodging."

Walker pulled out a suede-covered checkbook and scribbled for a moment, tore out the check, and handed it to Sable, whose eyes were wide with excitement. It was made out to Carter, who was advised the account be opened at a black bank if possible. He passed the check over to Niles, who looked at it in silence, his face expressionless as his eyes stared at the figure.

Thirty thousand dollars!

Niles passed the check around and turned to Walker.

"Why are you willing to do this? I mean, what's in it for *you*? Suppose we get caught, or worse yet, suppose they trace the money somehow to you. Look what you have to lose!"

Walker wasn't sure if he could answer the question. His mind was turning over reasons as fast as they appeared. He had been involved in questionable transactions before, but always for a profit. Niles was right. There was nothing in it for him but a headache if they got caught! He did have a lot to lose, but for some reason he felt a strange sense of pride at being involved in something so unique that the only return necessary was the personal satisfaction of knowing that they could play the game whitey's way and win.

It was a gamble he was willing to take, regardless of the consequences. Somehow the status he had obtained in medicine and community affairs seemed diminished in light of the discovery they had made. Any effort he could make in this venture would do more for black people than anything he had ever contributed in the past, only this time there would be no banquets of honor, no plaques of appreciation, no honorary degrees, no elections to boards of trustees, and no letters from the mayor.

He answered the question the only way he knew how.

"Niles," said Walker, settling himself comfortably into the contour of the couch, "you know, if the man ever gets the chance to use that concentration camp you found, he's not gonna be choosy. Doctors, lawyers, housewives, and junkies are all niggers to him. The only difference is the difference that we have created among ourselves. The man sees us *all* as niggers. That jail will hold me as well as it'll hold you!"

"Right on," said Sable. Rising from the couch, she clapped her hands in what would be the only acknowledgment of appreciation for his participation that Walker would ever get.

They adjourned at midnight and would not meet again until a search of the ghettos either yielded new information or proved to be a futile waste of energy.

CHAPTER 12

*T*HE SUMMER HEAT of August eased into the autumn breezes of September. Daylight began to end its reign prematurely, and trees once burdened with leaves of Kelly green now appeared naked against a hazy exhaust-filled sky. The summer reruns had ended, and the also-rans were beginning. "All in the Family" told it like it wished to be, and "Sanford and Son" told it like it was. The Rams looked promising, and the eyes of the world were on Hank Aaron.

Niles had worked diligently to coordinate an effort to search out the ghettos for evidence of underground prison camps. He lined up talent in each city selected and began the costly payoffs that would be necessary to acquire the explosives needed. The first target would be Chicago, a city where black folks and Cadillacs outnumber openings in the job market.

Carter received a call from Niles two weeks after their last meeting and found himself on a Continental 747 that same day. As he settled comfortably into the first-class seat, the thought of writing Sable struck him, and he released the seat-back and pulled down the table. As he began to write, another thought came into prominence, reflecting his real reason for wanting to come to Chicago. It had been a year since he had seen his children. Doby was seven and should look very much like him now. Cynthia was four and, well, she should look like her mother, petite and reserved. His preoccupation with remembering a part of his life torn from him paralyzed his hand, stopping the letter in midsentence.

Marsha Carter had panicked when he decided to leave the military. From a sheltered environment, she fled the subsidized embryo to her parents' home in Chicago. She had agreed to return only if and when he had settled himself and could prove there would be stability equal to that of the military. She begged him to return to the air force and eventually made it the only alternative to their reconciliation. Despite the pain caused by the separation, he felt he couldn't return, not even for her sake.

He tried Chicago briefly, but the agony of the winters and the stress of the pace were intolerable. He offered to take the children, in an effort to ease her responsibility, but she misinterpreted his actions and sought a divorce where visitation was restricted to a minimum. He supported them avidly and longed for the summers when they would stay with him. It would have been that way this summer had it not been for a maneuver on her part to keep them with her. No matter. He would surprise them by his presence.

Slight turbulence jogged him out of his painful memory, and he returned to the letter, finishing it as the stewardess announced over the PA system that the captain was beginning the descent into Chicago. He secured his seat belt and yawned several times to relieve the pressure in his ears. The squeal of the tires broke his concentration on the book he was reading as the jet touched down on the fog-enshrouded runway at O'Hare Airport. He took a bus to the Hilton Hotel downtown and rented a car for the drive to the South Side.

"Daddy, Daddy, Daddy," squeaked Cynthia as her tiny legs carried her into his arms at the bottom of the stairs of the dirty brick apartment house on South Calumet. She was as he last remembered her, effervescent, lively, and coquettish. Her round face and high cheekbones had filled out some since he had last seen her.

"Daddy, are you going to come and live with us again?" she said, her eyes flashing excitement as she searched his face innocently, looking for an affirmative answer. He held her tightly against him and swallowed hard several times to force the lump back down that was forming in his throat.

"Let's go see your mommy, OK?" he said as he carried her up the stairs to the entranceway. She wouldn't let him put her down and clung tenaciously around his neck as he waited for the door to open. Surprised, Marsha greeted him with disdain, having little to say during his entire visit. Doby joined them in the backyard equally excited as his sister about Carter's sudden presence. They spent the afternoon playing, laughing, and talking, the way he had always wanted it to be. Marsha served lunch, but did not eat with them.

He left, promising to call them daily and to see them again before he left for Los Angeles. He left Marsha a thousand dollars and a new insurance policy he had recently obtained. She was indifferent.

He would see her once more before leaving.

Returning to the Hilton, he unpacked and slept soundly until awakened by a phone call from Niles. He and Falcon were in the lobby, waiting. He dressed hastily and met them by the elevators ten minutes later. The trio drove to an apartment on the West Side of the city in the heart of the ghetto. They met with three men, identified only by nicknames, but who represented that they were from legitimate community agencies. Although dressed in clothes of the street, their diction and language betrayed a middle-class background. For what seemed like the millionth time they repeated the sequence of events to the men seated before them. As with Walker, there were many questions, but all three experts were eager to help.

Carter had taken a week's worth of vacation from the Center, confident that they would have their answer before it was time to return.

It soon became apparent that the task was monumental and

would require one of two things; either enlarging the search party or prolonging the time. They opted for the latter out of reasons of security. He extended his time three days, but when it still proved fruitless, he caught the first available flight home, stopping only briefly to say good-bye to the children.

He returned to Los Angeles both relieved and disappointed. He was relieved at not finding anything and disappointed for the same reason. It would take much longer than he had anticipated, and, because of work commitments, he would be unable to participate as planned. He spoke by phone periodically to Niles to keep himself current on their progress.

As September passed into October and October into November with its chilly evenings and mild days, Damon, and Leon found New York fascinating and, with some help from Carter, convinced their families to allow them to remain and attend school. Carter agreed to help subsidize them during their absence so as not to drain their families. He also felt it unnecessary to tell them about the discovery in the basement of the school or of their subsequent plans. He passed the search off as unproductive, their preoccupation with New York and trust in him having left them vulnerable to believe whatever he said. Although they had been straight with them, he felt their youth could not be trusted to keep secrets of this magnitude. He couldn't afford any leaks until it was over. Sable was in full agreement. Weeks went by with no word, and Thanksgiving passed to Christmas with its neon commercialism and postseason sales. Santa Claus brought black folks more cuts in the OEO programs and the elimination of the Model Cities work-study programs for underprivileged youth. New Year's Eve brought Guy Lombardo and Lawrence Welk into the homes of millions, while the funds for "Black Journal" were slashed so severely as to make the likelihood of viewing the program in the new year almost nonexistent.

The call came in January and awakened Sable out of a sound sleep. Carter had not arrived yet from the hospital where he was assisting on an appendectomy. She put on a pot of coffee and sat in the den to await his return. The sound of the electric garage door opener alerted her to his arrival, and she met him at the door adjoining the kitchen and the garage.

"Niles called a few minutes ago! Wants you to call him no matter what time you get in," she said, kissing him on the cheek as he entered.

"Did he say what he wanted?"

"No."

He hung up his coat, slipped off his shoes, and dialed the number scrawled on the pad while Sable poured him a cup of coffee. He relaxed in the recliner as he listened for a familiar voice to interrupt the monotonous, intermittent buzzing at the other end.

Niles finally answered, the half-sleepy voice recognizable throughout multiple yawns and repeated belching.

"Hey, nigger. Wake up—shit! It's . . ." He looked at his watch briefly, winding the mechanism as he talked. "It's four o'clock in the morning back where you are. What's so important you gotta talk to me this time of night? You worse than those kids a while back!"

"We hit the jackpot, baby, we hit the jackpot!" shouted the voice over the receiver. "We found one, in D.C., out in southeast under a junior high school! Same design as the one out there in L.A. No difference at all, except that it's a little bigger, but it's the same design!"

"No shit!" said Carter, motioning for Sable to sit next to him.

"You want me to come back there?" He cupped his hand over the phone and told Sable of the discovery.

"No, not yet at least. You know what this means? Man, Doc Walker was right on the money. I'm sure there are others we haven't found, but it's just a matter of time though. Mathis is down in Atlanta now talking to some people. I know they got one down there, as many niggers live in Atlanta!"

"What about Chicago?" Carter asked.

"Oh, it's there, all right, just can't find it. Got the city pretty much narrowed down now. It won't be long! Going to Philly and Bedford-Stuy next week to see how they doing." The audio on the phone began to fluctuate, making it difficult to hear.

"Speak up, Niles. I can't hear you!"

"Ain't no problem. I just wanted to tell you about it. We can talk again tomorrow during the day. Oh, and be sure to let your man know, will you? Later!" The dial tone returned to the receiver, and Carter placed it on the cradle. He sat motionless for a while, staring at the steam from the coffee as it teased his face with abandon.

"Can you imagine that! I bet they got 'em all over the country—shit! It wouldn't surprise me if there was *more* than one here in L.A."

"That's nerve, ain't it, baby?" said Sable, trying to be comforting.

"It's more than nerve; it's genocide, that's what it is! Goddamn genocide!" He started to dial Walker at home but hung up the receiver before he finished.

"I'll call him tomorrow. No sense waking him up this time of night just to ruin his dreaming." He looked at Sable and winked, drawing her close to him. She rested her head on his shoulder, saying nothing. He looked at the half-empty cup and placed it on the table.

"I'm tired, baby. Gonna hit the sack," he murmured.

"Me, too, honey," she said as she hooked her arm around his and walked slowly down the hallway to the bedroom where they would spend a restless night together.

The next time he heard from Niles he was in Los Angeles. Two more months had passed since that late-night phone call revealed the existence of another subterranean concentration camp. Niles called for a meeting that night, feeling that everyone's presence was necessary. At eight o'clock Leviah Walker pulled his Mark IV into the parking lot in front of Mafundi and joined what would be the last meeting they would ever have together.

Everyone was on edge as they waited for Niles to speak, his hand again massaging his beard as his eyes reviewed the notes in front of him. He began somberly.

"We should make no further phone calls to each other unless it's an extreme emergency. Is that clear?"

"Why?" asked Walker bluntly.

"Just as a precaution. We've done a lot of snooping around these past six months, and it may have raised some suspicions. Let's be on the safe side, OK?"

"If you say so."

"Now," began Niles, reshuffling his notes, "let me tell you where we're at. We have uncovered the presence of underground prison compounds in the following cities: Detroit, underneath a health clinic on the edge of the ghetto; in Chicago on the West Side beneath a Baptist church—and let me tell you about the church. The reason it took us so long to find the one in Chicago was because the preacher lives in the rectory. Man, let me tell you; preachers got the best hustle goin', *you* know. They don't have to go outside for nothin'. Women from the church bring 'em food, wash their clothes and, . . ."

"All right, Niles, that's enough bullshit, get on with the information," said Mathis. Niles shook his head and smiled, returned to his notes, and continued to read from the list.

"Let's see, where was I? Oh yes, in Bedford-Stuy underneath a tenement house; in Harlem, dig this! Underneath the new wing of Harlem Hospital, which, by the way, is the biggest we found, and it's a natural, you know why? Wheel niggers into the hospital, they just don't come out! Folks just figured they died!"

Sable felt chills run through her body as Niles continued to read from the list: "Newark, New Jersey, under a school; Washington, D.C., below a junior high school; Philadelphia, under a church on Girard Street, south side of the city; Baltimore, under a library adjacent to a police precinct; New Orleans, under a medical clinic; and in Atlanta, under a recently constructed day care center for children of working mothers, not far from Morehouse College."

When he finished, the room was silent, each person lost in his own thoughts. It had the most frightening implications for black folks; it was the first step in the final plan for the total elimination of black people from the society.

Niles took a seat in front of the filing cabinets and indicated that Falcon had some observations to share with the group.

"We checked into a few things the same as you did, Doc, and came up with the same exact thing. No architectural plans for the basement or anything like that. They used the same firm you mentioned, Carson-Porter. We did manage to locate one of the men who worked on the school project in D.C., a carpenter, but he said that they didn't get him involved until the basement was completed. He said that all construction workers were told not to go into the basement because of exposed high-tension wires, so they just never bothered. I'm sure that's the way it was with all of 'em.

"Also, the design of the corridors are identical to the ones here on 103rd Street, 'cept some are larger than others. You ought to see the one under Harlem Hospital—big-ass son of a bitch! Easily hold three or four thousand niggers! Each cell got four beds crammed into it. Same exact electrical system, too. Them motherfuckers pretty slick, fix it so as not to draw any power from the city 'lessen they wants to; that way they don't cause no suspicion. Them things could be there a hundred years, an' nobody'd ever know about it!"

Falcon continued: "Oh, yeah, in Harlem there's a tunnel with a small tram runnin' from the prison to the subway. They could move niggers in and out of there all day long, an' if they doin' what Doc says they is, about cuttin' on folks' brains an' all that, niggers be nothin' but vegetables when they get out!"

"What about the videotapes? You guys replace them each time?" asked Carter.

"Yeah, an' we ran the old ones to see if anyone had been there before us, but they were all blanks."

Walker, disturbed but not surprised at what they found, was more concerned about the appropriate expenditure of funds. He had to advance another twenty-five grand in January and had not received an accounting. Carter reassured him that the money was not wasted. He had monitored the checks as they came in and questioned Mathis when it was necessary.

Walker wanted to know more than that.

"What about arrangements for explosives?" he asked in a very businesslike tone.

"Got it all taken care of, Doc," said Niles, fishing in his pockets for a piece of paper with more information on it. He retrieved it and eyed Walker occasionally as he read.

"Got most of it from Canada but not as much as we needed.

Haven't found the jails in Oakland, Houston, or Boston as yet, so I guess we have enough to do away with the ones we got."

"Anyone get suspicious?"

"Don't think so. My contact man in Mexico is in the hospital for some reason, and I'm hesitant to talk with his replacement. Got plenty of dynamite and plastic explosives, but nitro is a bitch to get, mainly 'cause most folks don't know how to use it and are afraid of the stuff. One dude had to stop his truck and send for Mathis 'cause he got so scared! Shit like that is the only problem we run into."

"So when do they get blown up?" Walker snapped impatiently, constantly checking the time on his watch, its diamond-studded face sparkling in the light.

"That's the reason for the meeting, Doc, to decide how we gonna go about it!"

"What do you mean, decide how you're going to go about it? Just blow 'em up!" Walker, visibly irritated at what he thought was lack of preparation, began lashing out at them until Niles shouted him down.

"Shut up, Doc," yelled Niles, his temper beginning to show from behind the hairy mask, "and let me finish what I started to say, OK? You stick to medicine, and I'll stick to what I know best, and that's demolition!"

Walker gritted his teeth and looked contemptuously at Niles, pulling a cigarette out of a crushed pack of Kools.

"Like I said," Niles began, "the reason for the meeting is to work out a plan of action that will successfully put these damn things out of commission. Now the first question is, What do we do about the ones we haven't found? I mean after all, it takes three people weeks of painstaking work to cover an entire ghetto. You don't get no cooperation from people; you have to wait until they gone home, or on the weekends you wait till night. Shit! You cats don't know what it's like in the Jungle, believe me!" He waited for suggestions.

Sable was first, but her response lacked the insight needed to make it work: "Why don't we wait until we find all of them?"

"No way!" said Mathis, his burly frame stretched out on the floor next to the file cabinets. "Might take years to uncover all of them. Man probably have twice as many built by that time as there are in existence now."

"Not to mention the money it would cost, baby!" Walker mumbled softly.

"Why not blow the ones we have now, like a string of firecrackers one by one?" said Falcon.

"Yeah," responded Sable, her expression anxious for activity, "we could blow one a day until they're all eliminated."

Carter immediately saw the flaw in her thinking and countered.

"What do you suppose the man will do once he realizes the pattern? Shit, baby, once he recognizes that it's the concentration camps, he'll rush troops into every ghetto to protect the ones that haven't been dynamited. That's all we need!"

"*So,* what do *you* suggest?" asked Niles.

Carter thought a moment before speaking. Then, as if by divine revelation, he looked up and blurted out the answer impulsively: "Blow them all up at the same time!"

"All of them?" asked Falcon, needing clarification.

"Why not? It's the only way you can keep him from salvaging anything."

"But you just said that there are others we haven't found. What about them?"

"Right. But the man is concerned 'bout the niggers in the big northern ghettos. He ain't concerned 'bout the niggers in the South 'cause they living on farms and shit. But them ghetto niggers livin' close like that is the ones that he sees as a threat. You put his big-city concentration camps out of operation, and he'd be so immobilized it's unlikely he would attempt anything, 'cause he wouldn't want to tip his hand. Besides, he wouldn't have no place to keep all the niggers! I'm willing to bet he's got most of them in big cities."

Niles stroked his beard and thought pensively before he agreed. It did sound like the best alternative, but it would require locating and recruiting many demolition experts who could be trusted. It would take a while, but, yes, it could be done. In a month or two he felt they would be organized well enough to pull it off.

Walker still needed more assurance.

"How many men do you think it'll take, Niles?" he asked during a lull in the conversation.

"At least two for each facility. Smaller ones could probably be handled by one dude. The key is *where* the charges are set. Motherfuckers are built like a fortress; you don't place 'em in the right locations, all you got is a lot of smoke and burned walls! Need to set them at the leverage points, the supporting structures and the like."

"Are there that many brothers who know demolition?" Walker asked, genuinely interested.

"Oh yeah," Niles responded, "most of 'em came out of Nam. Some got jobs with construction companies, but most, like me, had to go back to the ghettos to make it the best way they could. Lots of 'em hustlin', pimpin', and whatever. You know the scene, man! I know a few who went back into the service, but not many. It's just a matter of *finding* them."

"What about money?" Walker asked cautiously.

"We still got about ten grand left. Should be enough to swing it! If not, I'll let you know through Carter."

"Chances are that you'll locate another facility by the time you're ready to blow these," said Walker, still the devil's advocate.

"I've thought about that, but it's a risk we'll have to take, I guess. If I have enough lead time, I can always spin a man off from one of the others and have him do it alone if necessary. I don't want to delay this thing any longer than is absolutely necessary."

They talked among themselves for another hour and then broke up. Niles would contact Carter when it was time; he didn't want anyone in the city when the action started. He and Mathis would coordinate the effort back east, but he would personally set the explosives in the facility on 103rd Street. Chances were that innocent people might be killed in the explosions, but they must try not to think about it. Many more might be killed if they didn't carry it off.

CHAPTER 13

MARCH PASSED INTO APRIL and April into May, like marathon runners pass the baton to the men ahead of them. The trees began to dress, as the warmth of spring announced the coming of summer. Birds, trying to rid their lungs of the sickness that would lead to their demise, flew in endless efforts to reach above the stagnant mass of polluted sky that covered the ghettos.

UCLA lost, and Arnold Palmer won. Whites continued to move to the periphery, leaving the central city a dying shell occupied by the poor, the sick, the black, and the aged. Black folks experienced the repossession of everything except their souls. The natural began to fade as corn-rowing appeared, and black folks once again were faced with the task of trying to define their identity.

Mathis and Niles worked around the clock to organize a task force of demolition experts. The talent was there, but the once-proud motivation was smothered in the despair and destitution that men often get when dreams and promises are dashed against the rocks of oppression.

Despite adversity, Niles had managed to assemble ten demolition men he felt were competent and committed. He held one last meeting with them in Chicago to set the date and the time. All facilities would be blown at six on a Monday morning. They would have to be extremely careful to remember the difference in time zones, lest one go off prematurely and alert the counterforces. He had to make three more trips across the country before returning to L.A. On the flight to Los Angeles he slept for the first time in two days, but it was not enough. Fatigue hovered over him as the plane touched down to the west on runway 27.

It was Sunday morning, and the airport was filled with commuter travelers from Oakland and San Francisco. He waited impatiently for a free phone, watching vacation travelers spend dime after dime to call relatives and friends they had just seen the week before. He rapped several times on the booth window where an adolescent white girl was fidgeting in her purse for another dime. She peered at him momentarily through the glass and left, slamming the door open in her indignation as she brushed past him.

Sable knocked the phone off the night stand as she fought to clear her disorientation. After what seemed an eternity Niles heard the half-asleep voice purr in the receiver.

"Sable? Niles! Get your old man on the phone for me. You folks got some tracks to make." A pause brought the hoarse voice of Carter to his ear.

"Wake up, man, and get the hell out of here! Call Leviah and tell him to get his butt on the road!"

"Where do you want us to go?" mumbled Carter through lethargic lips.

"Shit if I care. Just get the hell out of here! We're blowing the country tomorrow morning at six. Be sure to turn on your radio and listen to the honkies squirm. Man, oh, man, is the shit going to hit the fan now!" Niles was excited and could hardly keep his voice down in the booth.

By now his excitement was beginning to have its effect on Carter, who sat up in bed and wiped the sleep from his eyes. He slapped Sable hard across the buttocks as she slipped back into her dream.

"We'll be in Santa Barbara, OK? There's a small motel we usually stay in when we drive up the coast."

"I don't care where you stay, an' I sure don't want to know—just get on the road! Don't want you nowhere near this place, understand? I shouldn't even be calling you by phone, but I got too much to do today to see you in person. I'll be at Mathis's if you need to talk, but don't phone! Come down in person, understand? And not till *well* after it's announced on the air." Niles hung up the receiver without saying good-bye and hurried out of the airport to the valet parking where he kept his blue Ford from Hertz. He needed to sleep, but there was too much business to take care of before setting the charges later that evening.

Perhaps he could catch a nap in the afternoon.

By coincidence Walker was in Miami to attend a conference on infectious diseases, so he presented no problem. Carter and Sable dressed and had breakfast to the sounds of Jose Feliciano and John Coltrane. He advised his exchange that he would be out of town for a day or so and to please call the Center in the morning and alert them of his absence. After a brief, compulsive check of the house, he and Sable were nestled snugly in the cockpit of the Ferrari, her blue tote bag on the floor under her feet. He tried to talk her into leaving it behind, but she refused, stating it was a necessary piece of luggage for her wardrobe. He yielded, as only a chauvinist would.

The drive up the coast took two and one-half hours, longer than usual because Carter was in no particular hurry today. It would be a lazy drive, the splendid view from U.S. 101 was unparalleled; the thunder of white-capped waves crashing against the polished rocks at the base of sheer cliffs gave them a feeling that transcended the morbid existence they had in the city. This is what Carter enjoyed the most! This was his tranquilizer and martini combined: man and machine, free of the bonds of obligation and responsibility, if only for a day; free to roam the open spaces of the countryside that harbor secrets known only to the soil itself.

Settling into the motel, they had lunch and spent the balance of the afternoon walking arm in arm along the beach, the salty waves licking their ankles as they stood in the sand. He felt close to Sable, her soft body and revealing smile a warm combination that served to shore up a part of his life that had crumbled before his eyes, leaving him helpless and empty.

Sable's feelings were no less for him. As each day passed she felt it safer to reveal more and more of herself to him. She knew that he had been deeply hurt, but despite that, he had not allowed himself to suffer mistrust in her, and that quality alone let their relationship grow into what it was now, filling it with strength and affection because of their mutual respect for each other. She was glad she had met him and was beginning to feel as though she could stay with him forever.

As the tide moved closer to the shore and the sun set behind distant clouds, tainting the sky a golden yellow, they returned to the motel, where they ate and watched the Magnavox until the fatigue of the day weighted their eyes as a warning of the sleep soon to befall them. In defiance of it they found themselves embraced with one another as they made love one last time before falling exhausted, into the clutches of slumber.

Niles climbed the fence and made his way to the basement of the school for the last time. He carried a small satchel which contained the necessary material to demolish the school. It would be more than enough. He set the charges in strategic places almost by habit, as he had done a thousand times before, only for a different purpose and a different people. His eyes searched the gloom and followed the flashlight beam like a scout following a trail. As fatigue blurred his vision, he checked his watch. Two A.M., New York time! he thought, his mind still operating on Eastern Time.

In his exhaustion he had set his watch to Pacific Standard Time as soon as he had boarded the plane, but now the memory was lost behind too many nights without sleep and too many days with nothing but hotdogs and Cokes.

His mind still in New York, he set the armature of the timing mechanism back three hours to 11:00 P.M. and thus created the first flaw in what was to have been a sophisticated and almost perfect scheme.

Having finished with placing the charges, he extricated himself from the basement, made one last check of the yard, and bolted for the fence. He had decided against going back to the apartment, driving instead to the airport where he purchased a ticket for one of the hourly flights on PSA's evening shuttle to Oakland. In his haste he neglected to check the clocks that hung from the ceiling in the airport lobby, having just enough time to make the flight and seat himself before the door was closed.

He leaned back in the seat, closed his eyes, and listened to the distant whine of the engines as the 727 lifted itself into the darkness. He slept soundly until the repeated and annoying poking by the stewardess alerted him that the fifty-minute flight would be landing shortly. It was still dark when he walked out into the brisk foggy air in front of Oakland's terminal, where he hailed a cab and drove to the apartment where he always stayed when in the Bay Area.

Carter had left word that he would be unavailable over the weekend, but an urgent plea on the behalf of Mathis spurred his exchange to try several of his known favorite hide-aways in an effort to locate him.

As the phone rang violently on its cradle, Carter groped for the receiver. The moment he heard the operator's voice he knew something was wrong. Mathis was excited and concerned. The news media reported on multiple explosions throughout the country, but there was no mention of any similar activity on the West Coast. As Mathis chattered on the line, Carter turned the knob on the remote-controlled television tuner and waited for the snowflakes to appear. It was five after six, and the newscaster confirmed reports of several large explosions throughout the nation in the ghetto areas.

One commentator indicated that the FBI had been called in to investigate the possibility of a feud between the Mafia families. A noted civil rights leader stated that, since all explosions were in black areas, it was quite evident that white racists were trying to provoke the black communities into a confrontation with police. Several minor politicians, a senator, and two prominent labor leaders blamed antilabor forces with trying to disrupt the economy of the black communities in order to keep union representation from becoming effective in the ghetto. An unidentified representative from the school board in Washington, D.C., stated that there was definite evidence implicating antibusing foes as being primarily responsible for the destruction of the school in his city.

A Jewish rabbi, a Catholic priest, and two ministers from the Black Ministerial Alliance held a press conference in Chicago to protest what they felt were obvious religious overtones in the destruction of that city's ghetto church, all of which pointed to forces who feared the entry of the church into politics. The head of Atlanta's Welfare Subsistence Council protested the destruction of the day care center in that city's predominantly black area as a futile effort on the part of the radical element to block the flow of federal funds into the poverty areas of the South.

Much of Harlem Hospital's old unit was destroyed, and the new wing suffered extensive damage to the infrastructure. The head of the Black Hospital Administrators went on the air, stating that there was no longer any doubt that the white majority wanted all funds for national health legislation to go to white institutions instead of being disbursed to a segment of the population that also demanded quality health care.

The chairman for the Coalition for Quality Housing in Bedford-Stuyvesant openly attacked the absentee landlords who would rather destroy the existing housing than expend the monies needed to make the tenements livable. There was still no mention of any explosion in the Los Angeles area. Carter put through a call to a local radio station in the Santa Barbara area under the guise of being a naïve listener, and inquired about the possibility of any bomb activity in the state of California. The newsmen replied in the negative. He checked his watch—six-twenty. He placed several calls in an attempt to reach Niles and, after repeated failure, called one last number in Oakland and waited anxiously for the phone to answer.

Niles's drowsy voice crept through the receiver after some twenty-odd rings. "Did you set the charges yourself at the school?" snapped Carter, demanding an answer.

There was a pause as Niles tried to clear the cobwebs from his brain. The familiarity of the voice on the other end of the phone now established, he responded.

"Of *course* I did! Who *else* you think was going to do it? And besides, I thought I told you not to use the phone unless it was an emergency." The static in the receiver grew more intense, and they found themselves talking loudly to one another.

"This *is* an emergency, damn it!" said Carter, irritated at Niles's presumptuousness. "I've been checking out the news for the past thirty minutes or so, and they don't give any report of an explosion down in Los Angeles. What do . . . ?"

"Well of course not!" Niles quipped briskly, annoyed at the subtle questions about his competence. He glanced at his watch and, seeing the face report 6:30, quickly made the three-hour conversion to Pacific Standard Time and shouted, "It's only *three-thirty!* They ain't due to go off for another two and a half hours, but baby, when they do, *believe me,* you'll hear about it. I set it up real good!"

"Wait a minute, Niles. What *time* do you have? You just said two and a half hours—that would be nine o'clock in the morning!"

"Nope! Not set to go off at no nine o'clock. They're set to blow at *six* like I told you. It's three-thirty by my watch."

"Three-thirty?" screamed Carter. "Man, look at your watch again. It's six-thirty in the morning! Be daylight in a few minutes!"

"Six-thirty?" There was a short silence, but Carter could hear Niles moving about in the room and then suddenly the sound of music blared through the receiver. Niles reduced the volume and turned the dial until he found a station with the morning news. Carter heard the announcer give the time as 6:40 A.M. Then he heard Niles pick up the phone again.

"Oh, my God!" shouted Niles through the receiver, *"my watch was right all along!* I don't remember ever setting it before I went into the school, but I must have done it on the plane. *Damn!"*

"So what does that *mean?*" asked Carter, near hysteria.

"I was so tired last night. The timing mechanism is set to go off at six, but that means nine, because I set it back three hours from Pacific Standard Time, but I thought it was New York time!"

Carter checked his watch again. "Are you absolutely sure, man?"

"Yeah, yeah, I'm sure, 9:00 A.M. instead of 6. I'm sure now!"

"That means the school will be full of kids—shit! Every last one of 'em will be *killed!*"

"From where I am I'd never make it down there to reset the goddamn charges! Can you get down there in time to get those kids out of that place? Motherfucker's gonna blow sky high! Take the whole block with it and then some!"

"Yeah, I can get there if I leave ten minutes ago!" said Carter as he slammed down the receiver and jumped out of bed to dress. Sable, having heard the entire conversation, followed suit.

"Baby," said Carter moving toward the door, "if we don't get there by nine o'clock, there's gonna be two thousand dead children and a half-million angry niggers! *Let's move it!*"

Sable grabbed her tote bag and purse, whisking herself into the front seat of the car just as Carter snapped the clutch, lurching it backward out of its parking spot. He wheeled the Ferrari out of the parking lot and onto the main highway, heading south, smoke pouring from the ground as the tires spun in vain effort to grip the pavement. The response of the engine was sluggish because it was cold, and the disk brakes, not yet warm to temperature, gripped poorly.

They headed south toward Pacific Coast Highway through patches of early morning fog that collected on the coast during the night, as the cool moist air flowed across ground still warm from the previous day's sun.

"Damn," said Carter as he eyed the gas gauge, the needle sitting on "Empty." "Didn't bother to fill up 'cause I hadn't planned on coming back this soon."

He checked his watch—six-fifty! Reducing his speed, he searched frantically for a gas station that was open, his eyes sweeping the road from side to side through the fog. After passing three closed stations, he spotted a small independent on the far side of the highway. Without looking, he spun the Ferrari around in the middle of the street and raced for the pumps.

The attendant was a youngster, fresh out of high school, who was more interested in talking about automobiles than he was in servicing them. After several minutes of irritating chatter, Carter jumped from the car and grabbed the pump from the youngster's hand, but he recoiled.

"That's all right, mister, I'll do it! Don't be in such a hurry."

"Yeah, well *do it,* then, instead of talking about it!"

The youngster glared at him a moment and angrily thrust the nozzle into the filler neck to feed the sleeping beast. Carter paced anxiously next to the pumps then walked back to the car and stood beside Sable, nervously tapping his fingers on the low-slanted roof as he watched the dials spin like pinwheels on the gasoline pump.

"Motherfucker sure takes long enough just to fill a goddamn tank!" said Carter, wiping the residue of sleep from his tired eyes. Sable reached through the window and affectionately rubbed his arm as it rested against the roof of the car.

"Try not to worry about it, baby. It'll be all right. We'll make it."

"Yeah, well I'll feel a lot better once I get on the road. How's the time?"

"Seven exactly."

"Damn!"

Carter turned his attention to the street just in time to see the black Plymouth from the highway patrol pass by and make a U turn in the middle of the intersection a block from the station. The patrol car made another pass at a much slower speed, its occupants drawn by the presence of a black man next to what was quite obviously a very expensive vehicle. They made another U turn at the same exact spot where Carter had turned and pulled slowly into the station behind the Ferrari.

They disengaged themselves from their seats and, upon leaving the cruiser, adjusted their gun belts and positioned the holsters in a show of bravado. They approached the Ferrari on the driver's side, circling it in a counterclockwise maneuver. They resembled Mutt and Jeff. The older and more-experienced-appearing cop was tall and heavy, his eyes set deep in his face, his nose a bulbous protrusion above a shirt that didn't quite fit. The younger cop was short and thin and reminded Carter of a marine recruit. He had freckles, a close-cropped military-style haircut, and spoke with a slight southern drawl.

"This your car?" he asked, his hand resting comfortably on the butt of his revolver. The taller cop indicated that he would assume the interrogation and waved his partner back to the cruiser.

"Now, like he said, is this your car?"

"Yes, it's mine. Why?"

"I'll ask all the questions if you don't mind. Let me see your license and registration!" He stood directly in front of Carter, both hands on his hips, his teeth slowly masticating a toothpick. He spoke in usual police jargon and manner, condescending, insulting, and, above all, provocative. The sight of Carter next to the sleek Ferrari was more than he could bear. Carter handed him the license.

"Is there a problem, officer?" he asked in the most benign and humble attitude he could muster.

176

"Yeah," came the reply, "you were born!"

Carter bristled, stood erect, and looked the cop in the eye, his rage boiling. "What did you say, man?"

The sudden change in attitude from subservient to aggressive was unexpected, and the cop returned Carter's stare with equal intensity, his arm hanging loosely by the holster as he rapidly opened and closed his fist to work the stiffness out of his fingers. He turned to walk toward the cruiser and, as he did so, removed the nightstick from its belt, holding it ominously as he moved to the rear of the Ferrari.

"You wait right here, boy! Don't move an inch!"

"What?"

"You heard me!"

Sensing the cop was already irritated and looking for any excuse to break open his head, Carter bit the bullet and remained by the car. "This motherfuckin' honky is *crazy!*" he mumbled to Sable as she got out of the car. "I haven't done *anything!* What the hell is wrong with them? Are they stupid or something?"

"Shhh," said Sable, "we don't have time to play games with them. If he's going to give you a ticket, let him give you a ticket— shit! It's seven-ten already—just be cool so we can get the hell *out* of here!"

"That motherfucker gonna get his ass kicked, he keep talking to folks like that—shit!"

"Really," Sable agreed.

The gas station attendant finished filling the tank and asked for his money. Carter handed him a crisp ten-dollar bill and told him to keep the change. The boy regarded him strangely for a moment, somehow managed a smile, and returned to the office. Carter walked to the driver's side of the car and waited for the cop to make his next move.

"Hey, come here!" yelled the cop, his face flushed with contempt.

Well, at least I've moved from boy to no name, Carter thought to himself as he approached the car cautiously, keeping a wary eye on his partner perched against the door on the passenger side.

"You a *doctor?*" the cop asked sarcastically.

A broad grin broke on Carter's face. Finally, the hassle would be over now; the title would protect him as it had always done.

"Yes."

The cop shook his head and stared at the license a moment. "They just let you people do anything nowadays, don't they? It's a goddamn shame!"

"You know, buddy, I don't like your attitude. I've been stopped all over this country, North and South, but I've never run across anyone as foul as you!" said Carter, incensed. The cop pushed open the door and stood up, ready for war.

"Foul?" the cop questioned loudly. "Nigger, you're the last person to ever say that to me. Now you got a warrant 'cause you didn't pay a ticket back in August, an' I got a mind to run you in for it!" Carter stared into space, trying to remember.

"Don't try and give me that I don't remember shit, 'cause it don't work with me! I was going to give you a break, but you got such a bad mouth." He paused to answer a call on the radio and, when finished, resumed his tirade of ignorance. "Goddamn nigger doctors figure you can get away with shit!" he said, blowing his stale breath in Carter's face.

"You go wait by the car till I'm ready for you," he said, getting back in the cruiser and grabbing the microphone. Carter backed away from the car and walked slowly toward the Ferrari, his mind still trying to remember that day in August that threatened to block his only chance of warning the school. He returned to the Ferrari, joining Sable, who leaned comfortably against the fender.

"Don't do that, baby. It's aluminum, and it'll bend."

Sable looked at him peevishly a moment, then moved off the fender, hooked his arm with hers, and affectionately planted a kiss on his neck.

"Motherfucker says I got a warrant; a ticket I never paid since last summer. I can't remember any ticket I haven't had taken care of!"

"You sure?"

"Damn right I am! Always get Ellis to do it."

"Who's Ellis?"

"Don Ellis, the attorney. He always fixes 'em for me. I ain't never had to go to no court!"

"Maybe he goofed this time."

"Oh *bullshit!* He would've called me and said so if that were the case."

"What's the pig gonna do?"

"Says he might run me in. Can you believe that shit? Of all the times for shit like this to happen!"

"Can't you talk him out of it?"

"Not that honky—bastard is typical cracker, from his heart." As they talked, the first rays of morning crept over the mountains and painted the landscape in misty white. Carter checked his watch—seven-fifteen!

"Hey look, baby, if I go to the jailhouse, you get to the school and warn the principal about what's happening. Get him to empty that school any way you can. Use your rod if you have to, but do it!"

Sable, feeling uncomfortable about the events as they were unfolding didn't help the situation any. "I can't drive a stick. You know that!" Carter cursed under his breath, and, shaking his head, lit a cigarette, still thinking of alternatives against the rapidly eroding time remaining.

Even without the sparse makeup she normally wore, Sable was an enticement to any man who saw her. Today was no exception, and though she had dressed hastily and neglected to comb her natural, she looked strangely appealing, silhouetted against the reflected glare of the haze. The young cop standing passively beside the cruiser had eyed her constantly since their arrival. As Carter returned to the driver's side of the car to retrieve additional cigarettes from the sun visor, the cop made a tactical error in standard law enforcement procedure; he left the cruiser and moved toward Sable, now standing alone.

"You married to him?" he asked sarcastically, snapping his head in Carter's direction.

Sable drew her purse up tightly under her arm and responded, looking through him with an empty stare.

"I don't think that's any of your business!" she snapped and turned to get back in the Ferrari. His play rebuffed, the cop grabbed her tightly by the arm and jerked her toward him.

"I'm talking to you, *black bitch!* Don't ever turn your back on me when I address you! Goddamn niggers think you better 'n white folks just 'cause you got a little education and money. . . ." He glared at her a moment and released her arm, pushing her away. He had done as his forefathers had done centuries before him when their fantasies about black women could no longer be contained.

This was not the first time that Sable had been subjected to the indignities of white men, but it would be the last.

"Don't ever touch me again, honky. You understand?"

"What? Don't ever—?" the cop stood smiling cynically. Her response excited him ever more.

"I said, don't ever touch me again, honky—! You ain't deaf!"

Carter was enraged and started around the front of the car for the cop, but the cop came with instant paranoia and a two-second reflex, his fingers tightly gripping the butt of the gun that hung on his side. He extended his arm and provocatively pointed a finger toward Carter's face.

"You don't go *nowhere,* boy!" he said, fingering the trigger. Carter froze by the fender, his anger about to explode. The cop moved for Sable again.

"Bitch! I ought to slap the living shit out of you for talking back to me." He reached for her arm again, but she jerked it out of range, drawing him closer to her. She slowly and subtly fingered the zipper on the purse, withdrawing the six-inch switchblade that had been her constant companion for years.

"You black . . . ." The cop removed his hand from the revolver and reached again for her arm. The click of the extended blade registered as he tried to block her movement, but it was too late, Sable twisting the handle as she plunged it deep into his abdomen.

The cop staggered back from the car in shock, his mouth hanging open, his eyes wide, and his hands clasped over his stomach as blood poured from the wound. As he spun around toward the street, his knees buckled, dropping him to the pavement. His body writhed in pain as a stream of blood flowed past his head and down the driveway into the street.

Carter stood immobilized, his eyes fixed on the twitching form that lay on the ground. Gathering his senses, he looked toward the cruiser, but the other cop had been too preoccupied with procedure and missed the stabbing. They moved for the car in unison, Sable folding the blade back into its handle.

Not until he heard the whine of the engine and the scream of the tires did the cop in the cruiser look up. The Ferrari whipped out of the gas station past the slain officer, across the painted highway divider, and down the fast lane of traffic until hidden by the steel dividers three blocks away.

The cop jumped out of the cruiser and ran to his partner, gun in hand. Seeing it was useless to try and shoot, he returned to the car, radioed for an ambulance, and requested an all-points bulletin on the fugitives as he cranked the big 490-cubic-inch V-8 in preparation for pursuit.

Carter developed a good lead on the Plymouth as he moved swiftly down the highway in the early morning fog that dotted the coast. Leaving the city limits, he began to put the Italian prancing horse through its paces. The engine warm and the brakes sure, he felt it safe to push the car to its limits. He slithered in and out of traffic like a snake between rocks. Approaching a notorious curve just outside of Port Huyneme, Carter overjudged his speed, had to brake hard, and sent the car in a 45-degree spin. As the Ferrari turned sideways and slid along the road toward the outside shoulder, Carter turned the wheel in the direction of the spin and released the brakes in an effort to realign the chassis. As he approached dangerously close to the edge of the road, the car began to straighten out its direction, and as it did so he threw it into second gear, mashed the accelerator hard to the floorboard, and whipped the car around the curve as smoke seeped from the fenderwells.

The fog increased, making it necessary to slow his speed considerably. He checked his watch compulsively—seven-twenty-five. They had an hour and a half to cover a distance that normally took two to two and a half hours. He scanned his gauges like a computer, oil pressure held at 90 pounds, oil temperature holding at 140, and tach sitting on 7,500. Reaching a clear area in the highway, he once again opened the cage and the sleeping beast emerged to exercise its limbs. As he went through the gears, the tone from the exhaust changed pitch with each shift. Normally it would be music to his ears, but now it was a matter of life and death; the car had to perform flawlessly. The speedometer inched toward 150 as the road before him became narrow, his acuity now demanding perfection lest an error in judgment create disaster.

The Plymouth was not to be taken lightly, its high compression and special carburation propelling the Detroit tank equally fast. Only in cornering did the Ferrari have the advantage; its unique design followed the turns as though held to the road by some unknown force. As he topped 150 Carter noticed for the first time the absence of the vibration in the steering mechanism as the body settled comfortably on the chassis. He kept one eye on the rear-view mirror as if he could magically prevent the Plymouth from catching him; its red light was now barely visible in the distance. His heart pounding as fast as the engine, he struggled to think ahead to the next curve, the next dip, the next road block as beads of perspiration rolled off his forehead and settled into his lap.

For the first time since they had left the gas station Sable spoke, her mind turning over and over the events leading up to her present predicament.

"Goddamn honky cop made me sick! White-ass mother-fucker!" she sneered wiping the blood from the blade of the knife with her handkerchief.

"Do you think he's dead, baby?" Carter asked.

"I hope so!" She folded the blade into the handle and placed it in her purse. "Last time that son of a bitch ever puts his hands on *me!*"

Carter whipped the Ferrari around another curve and found himself sitting behind a diesel truck. He checked the time—seven-thirty-five. The lumbering truck flashed its running lights, signaling Carter to pass. He did so and found himself at the end of a string of cars following another diesel.

"Oh, Christ! This is all I need!" he shouted in desperation. "Come on, come on, pull over or something—shit!" He checked the rearview mirror. It was empty.

"That cop'll be right on top of me if I don't get around these fools."

Sable tried to be supportive. "Just cool it, baby. Don't panic."

Carter remained silent, his eyes glued to the rear-view mirror. After reflecting a moment in silence, he spoke.

"You know what all this means, don't you?" he asked somberly, taking his eyes off the road.

"Yeah, it means we got"—she looked at her watch briefly—"exactly an hour and twenty minutes or so. Just keep driving."

"That's not what I'm talking about, baby, and you know it!"

She reached across the seat and touched his arm, her fingers gently massaging his tense muscles under the cotton sweater. She sighed, lit a cigarette, and stared pensively at the dancing flame before blowing it out.

"Yeah, I know what it means, honey. If they catch us I'll go up for murder and you'll be prosecuted as an accessory. That's why we have to get to the school in time, to make it all worthwhile. I mean, don't you see, baby? The man ain't never gonna let black folks alone. They keep beating you down until you have no initiative left, no motivation to do anything 'cept live from day to day. Well, damn it, those kids have got to have a chance to make it better than we did!"

"But Sable, what do we do with our lives after it's all over, the school thing I mean?" he asked, his eyes darting from hers to the road to the mirror.

"I know what you're thinking," she said. " 'I'm Mr. Middle-Class Nigger! I've worked hard, accumulated material wealth. Why throw it all away?' Hey, baby, it don't work like that! You *think* you got everything. Well let me tell *you* something! You don't have your freedom! That thing back there with the pigs should tell you that! You don't have *shit!*"

"I never thought it would end like this," he said sadly.

"Its the only way it could have ever ended for us," she said calmly, her voice confident and unafraid. "We knew it was a gamble when we started, but the dice came up with snake eyes. Bingo! We lose. The man stacked the deck in the very beginning. We called his bluff; he don't like that at all! Besides, we got . . ."

The sudden blast from a high-pitched air horn interrupted the conversation, accompanied by the constant rasping sound of an engine being revved repeatedly. In the mirror Carter could see the familiar shape of a yellow Porsche 911-S. His attention once again turned to the road; the line of cars had dwindled, placing him next in turn to pass the diesel. He started to move to the passing lane, but the Porsche blocked him, having pulled up alongside, its occupants waving their hands out of the window in a gesture indicating a desire to race.

Carter pulled abruptly back into his lane and waved them off, but the Porsche continued to beep the horn and darted in front of the Ferrari.

"That fool wants to race! Any other time I'd be willing—what time is it?"

"Seven-forty-five. Can't you get around this truck?"

Carter moved to the outside once again, but the Porsche did likewise, obviously an intentional move to keep the Ferrari behind the truck. At the last minute the Porsche pulled ahead of the diesel as oncoming traffic filled the passing line. They were on a downhill grade moving at a snail's pace, the road twisting and turning in a serpentinelike fashion. Patches of fog continued to line the road, weaving a quilt of land and mist that settled quietly over the countryside, its serenity broken only by the sounds of grinding engines and blaring horns.

The narrow, two-lane grade ended, and the road became a four-lane highway once again. As Carter pulled to the outside to pass the diesel, he caught a glimpse of the Plymouth in the mirror, its red light ominously clear in the distance. They had lost valuable time behind the truck, and the only hope of putting any distance between them and the Plymouth would be to reach the mountains again with its sharp-canted turns and narrow pavement.

Sable turned to see the Plymouth through the rear window. "That pig is closing in on you, honey. Can't you lose him?"

"I would have if it hadn't been for that goddamn truck and those crazy kids in the Porsche! He's got too many horses for me to lose him on the straight, but I can eat him alive in the mountains!"

The driver of the Porsche could see Carter bearing down on him and started to move to the outside lane to block him when he saw the red light in the distance. He quickly returned to his previous lane and reduced his speed as rapidly as possible without being obvious. The vacuum created by the tremendous speed differential as the Ferrari and the Plymouth passed the Porsche made it shimmy in their wake. Like ballet dancers, the cars nimbly moved from lane to lane as they sought to avoid the slower-moving vehicles.

"This traffic is a bitch! Every fool in the world must be going to work!"

"Lotta black folks would like to be doing that, too!" Sable retorted, her eyes still fixed on the red light behind them.

Carter's hands began to sweat as the Plymouth drew nearer. The cop also knew that he would have to pull ahead of the Ferrari before they reached the mountains. He pulled up behind the Dino and drafted the car, nose to tail, down the highway. As they reached the end of the straight section just before the highway narrowed to a single lane, the cop tried to pull alongside the Ferrari and force it off into the soft shoulder of the road, but Carter downshifted, braked hard, and set the Dino up for the apex of the curve. The sudden move scared the cop into hitting his brakes prematurely, sending the Plymouth into a 360-degree skid, narrowly missing the center divider and coming to rest on the soft shoulder. Surprised at finding himself intact and the car undamaged the cop returned to the pavement and took up the chase.

The surefooted Ferrari moved with ease through the winding turns as pockets of fog hung menacingly over the ridges, blocking their view to the ocean. As quickly as he had entered the mountains, Carter found himself on flat land again with the Plymouth fast approaching. Sable glanced at the tote bag and again out the rear window.

"How do you take the top off?" she asked.

"What?"

"The top! How do you take the top off?" she repeated, pointing to the roof with her finger.

"It's like a 'Vette, has two panels. It's not a single roof. Why?"

"Don't worry about it. Just tell me how to take the top off on my side." Reluctantly, he described the latches and the lever that actuated them. She disengaged her seat belt and maneuvered into position under the lever, pulling it hard to the left. Caught by the wind, the top flew off and careened down the highway toward the side of the road. A sudden gust of wind filled the void as Carter fought to control the lurching car, now in disequilibrium with the environment.

"This is going to slow us up. Don't handle the same with the roof off." Sable wasn't listening. Her attention was fixed on the Plymouth, now only several car lengths behind them.

"Slow up a little more, honey. Let him get right up on you."

"Shit, baby, I don't have a choice. Goddamn car handles like a *truck* without the top! What the hell you up to?"

"Slow up a little more." Sable reached into the tote bag, removed the Baretta, and loaded the clip. As the Plymouth tucked in behind them she released the safety and maneuvered her arm through the narrow opening. She peered out of the hole, her eyes at roof level as she began to align the pistol. The cop, sensing what was about to happen, backed off and weaved from side to side, but it was too late. Sable squeezed off two shots in rapid succession. The first was too high, but the second smashed through the window, striking the cop in the temple and sending the patrol car veering across the double yellow line and head-on into a diesel tractor-trailer rig, exploding on impact.

Sable took a deep breath and fell back into the seat, dropping the gun out of the car, as the Ferrari disappeared once again into a fog bank. It seemed strangely quiet now as the cool moist air whistled through the car. Sable pulled her sweater tightly around her neck as the chill of the fog enveloped her. Her watch indicated seven-fifty-five!

"You got any heat in this thing?"

Carter closed the vent and turned on the fan, sending a blast of warm air into her lap. She relaxed and began counting the minutes to herself.

It was foggy clear into Malibu, and eight o'clock found them on the outskirts of the city.

"Gotta ditch this car before the fog lifts, baby. Otherwise, we'll never get into L.A. Every cop in the state probably on to us by now."

"Let's go to a motel," said Sable as she leaned across the seat and twisted his watch to cross-check the time.

"Why?"

" 'Cause you'll probably find a car with keys in the ignition."

"It's worth a try."

"Really is!"

Carter pulled the Ferrari into a small motel that was set back from the main highway. Sable's idea proved to be a prophecy. As they drove slowly around in the gray mist, Sable noticed a Camaro idling outside the front of the motel. Its occupants were still checking out in the lobby, so Carter parked the Ferrari and moved for the Camaro on the distant side. They entered through the driver's side, Carter releasing the emergency brake and letting the car coast down the driveway so as not to alert the owners.

They moved silently through the fog of Malibu, its hillside estates and year-round playhouses sitting hidden on the other side of tomorrow. They moved past the highway patrol office and down the short stretch of road that led to the Santa Monica Freeway. His watch showed eight-twenty. The traffic was at its worst as cars fought for an inch at a time. When they reached the Harbor Freeway, Carter decided to use the city streets, fearing the congestion would be worse on the freeway. It was a legitimate concern. He turned off at Adams Boulevard and headed east toward Central Avenue, running red lights when he felt it safe to do so. He drove down side streets, cross streets, and alleys, the Camaro a poor excuse for a performance car. The character of the city began to change as they drew nearer to the school. Business establishments grew sparse, liquor stores grew frequent, and the residents grew naturals. It was eight-forty when they reached 103rd Street and the sights became familiar; past the 103rd Street Precinct, the vacant lots, the old station by the tracks, the vacant lots again and Mafundi, where it all began.

The school loomed in the distance as a majestic monument to one of man's most horrendous plans.

It was eight-fifty!

CHAPTER 14

ARTER PARKED THE CAMARO on Anzac Street, grabbed Sable by the hand, and raced across the street to the school. Bursting into the front office, they sat momentarily in two of the wooden chairs that lined the wall facing a bevy of secretaries responsible for the operation of the school. The young woman seated adjacent to the door at the far end of the office regarded the two panting figures curiously as she motioned for them to approach her desk.

"May I help you?" she said and smiled, her curiosity over-whelming.

"Yes. Where's the principal? We've *got* to see him!" Carter said between breaths.

"Well I *am* sorry, sir, but Mr. Racker doesn't see parents without an appointment. If you'll leave your . . ."

Carter noticed the sign on the door next to her desk with the word "Principal" neatly engraved on its surface. Pulling Sable by the arm, he rushed past the secretary and pushed through the door over her very loud and very foul protest.

"Nigger, you can't go in there. . . ."

Carter ignored her and closed the door in her face as she tried to follow them through to the office.

The sign on the desk said: DAVID MARTIN RACKER, PRINCIPAL. He stood abruptly as he had done many times before when parents entered without an introduction, not quite certain of what to expect. Racker was short, white, slightly balding, and wore button-down shirts with frayed collars. He stood before them with an air of arrogant grandiosity, quite unlike the portrait of Lincoln that hung on the wall behind him. His voice was deep and his mannerism garish. He fancied himself, like Lincoln, a man who had come to the ghetto to free the slaves.

"I would appreciate it if you would knock before entering next time," he said, his voice ringing with a distinct nasal tone. Sensing the irritation of the couple before him, he discontinued his tongue-lashing and offered them seats next to the American flag that hung from a pole located in a corner of the room.

"What is your child's name?"

"*A bomb! A bomb! There's a bomb in the basement!*" shouted Carter between breaths, pointing toward the floor with his hand.

"A bomb? Are you sure? I mean, how do you know?"

Carter cringed at the thought of having to explain it to him. "It's due to go off"—he looked at the clock on the wall—"in *seven minutes*. You gotta get these kids *out* of here!"

The principal rose from his seat and pushed the intercom button, signaling for the secretary to enter the office.

"There's a jail under the school, and it's gonna get blown up. Please get these kids out of here!"

At that point he looked at them, and a sickening smile crossed his face as he sat back down. He placed the tip of his pencil between his teeth and swiveled sideways.

"A *bomb*, you say," he said facetiously, swinging back toward them like a barbie doll. "Is that a fact?"

Carter checked the clock again and began to plead with Racker until he realized how he must have sounded. Sensing his mistake, he motioned for Sable to follow and bolted from the office, jarring the secretary as he brushed past her.

"What was *that* all about, Mr. Racker?"

"Some nut trying to tell me there's a prison under the school with a bomb in it. Craziest thing I ever heard! Poor fellow must have lost his mind. Pity his wife, though—she seemed so helpless. His insane babbling must have embarrassed her considerably."

He turned to reenter the office and caught himself, wheeled back around, and ordered the secretary to place a call to the police and alert them to potential trouble from a lunatic.

In the hallway, Carter was desperate. His thoughts were blank. He had run out of ideas. He felt like shouting in each classroom, but he knew they would look at him like a fool. Suddenly Sable nudged him in the side with her elbow.

"What, baby? Don't bother me now. I've got to think of something to get these kids out of here. I . . . ." His voice was lost in the ringing of the five-minute warning bell as the screams and laughter of innocent children filled the hallway.

"*The fire alarm,* the fire alarm! *Break the fire alarm!*" she yelled, pulling him in the direction of the red box fastened on the wall in front of them. Instinctively Carter smashed the glass with his fist and pulled frantically on the white lever in the center.

Dazed, he rested his head against the wall, his hand frozen to the lever as he listened to the sweet sound of the intermittent ringing of the bells as the classrooms emptied into the hallways and onto the playground. But the procedure was unrehearsed and chaotic; the indifferent staff, confused and disoriented. Children scattered about with no direction, enjoying what they considered to be a game.

He sent Sable out to the playground to help the teachers get the children beyond the perimeter of the schoolyard, then returned to the basement in an effort to find the charges so as to reset the timing devices and buy an extra five minutes.

Finding the door easier than anticipated, he moved through the narrow opening and into the darkness of the anteroom. He fumbled for the switch next to the entranceway and forced the inner door ajar. He would have time! Where did Niles place the charges? In the electrical panel? No! He said in strategic places. Yes, *that's it!* Strategic places like support columns—but what are support columns? He searched frantically, his heart pounding, his breathing rapid and shallow, his hands shaky and tremulous, his mind spinning! Where to *look?* Which corridor, which cell? Oh God, Niles, where did you put them?

Sable had managed to convince some of the teachers the urgency of removing the children beyond the fence. They swarmed into the streets of the ghetto and onto the porches and sidewalks of its residents. She looked at her watch: it was nine! *No explosion!* Niles must have been off a few minutes, but where's Carter? He should have been out by now! The school is empty. Why isn't he out yet? Oh, baby, please get out of there. Please, honey, *now!*

As the terminal feeling began to creep over her, she screamed hysterically and began running toward the school. "Baby, please get out of there before it's too late, please . . . !" Her words were lost in the deafening sound of the explosion as the ground convulsed and columns of black smoke billowed upward toward the sky. The classroom building crumbled like a matchbox as the blacktop caved in; the air filled with flying debris. She sank to her knees in a daze, crying uncontrollably as glass shattered around her. A pair of strong arms encircled her and pulled her to safety behind a tree. For a moment she thought, Yes, it must be! But as she looked around to see her benefactor, she saw it was a woman, a nameless face in the ghetto.

She continued to stare but saw nothing; children around her were crying, but she could not hear them; people behind her were in pain, but she had no feelings. She was alone again.

Numb with shock, she somehow managed to pick herself up from the ground and began walking toward 103rd Street across the debris and broken glass that lay in her path. She didn't hear the shouts of people warning her to take cover. She had no thoughts other than to leave. She had no sense of direction, no plan. She just wanted to *leave*—drive anywhere, go anyplace—but *leave!* It didn't matter anymore now that she was alone. Life no longer held any meaning for her.

The explosion left 103rd Street in shambles. Storefront windows were broken, and the street was littered with glass and bricks. There were numerous injuries and a score of fatalities. She walked bleakly past several bodies, their lifeless forms unrecognizable in the clutter of the street. Anzac had been spared, and the Camaro was undamaged. Dogs roamed the street hesitantly, and infants cried in the confusion.

The sound of sirens filled the air and became distant as she drove west. "Why, why, why, Niles? You didn't have to make the mistake! You could've set the time correctly, *damn you!* You didn't have to *kill* him! He was all I had, the only one I cared about! He didn't have to die this way, not like *this!* It was all so unnecessary, so unfair! He deserved better than this!"

Her mind blank and empty, she drove instinctively to the airport, parked in front of the taxi stand, left the engine running, and ran inside the International Terminal. She pushed her way indifferently through the crowd until she reached the counter of Aeronaves Mexico.

Clutching her purse tightly, she released it only when the ticket salesman asked for her credit card.

"Are you all right, miss?" he asked sincerely.

"Yes, yes. I was just thinking, that's all. Thank you."

"Here's your ticket, miss. Boarding at gate three today. The main ramp is out of order, so you will have to board from the ground exit to your right. Do you have any bags?"

"None."

"Very well. You still have about ten minutes before flight time, but I suggest you board now for a better seat selection."

"Thank you, I will." She walked the length of the passenger terminal and stepped on the horizontal escalator. It moved slowly and steadily toward the boarding gate.

Her concentration was broken by the voice of the man at the security station.

"May I have your purse, please?"

"What?—oh—I'm not ready to board just yet, thank you." She backed away and walked toward the ladies' room, where she disposed of the knife and made a weak attempt to reapply her mascara, but the tears wouldn't stop, and she found herself momentarily paralyzed with grief.

Gathering her remaining strength, she returned to the security gate, checked her purse, and crossed the pavement to the boarding ramp. The plane would be in Mexico at four. She would have time to think, time to plan her life. Oh, God, he didn't have to die this way!

As she moved slowly up the stairs of the ramp, she felt a slight pain in the back of her throat as the world started spinning around her. Things became hazy then dark. Blood spilled out of her mouth as she tumbled down the metal stairs and lay sprawled on the concrete, her lifeless form oozing blood from the back of her neck where the bullet found its mark.

It was over.

192